"I Hate It When You're Mad at Me, Marybeth"

"You're such a rat," she said weakly.

"Hillary's fun to be with as a friend," he said. "But you're my girl. You know that."

She smiled, blind to anything but the sound of his coaxing voice.

"Look," he said, and took her hand. In the snow he had traced a heart with the toe of his boot. Now he drew their initials inside the heart. "There we are," he said.

"What about when the snow melts?"

"Someday I'll get you a ring," he promised.

"Oh, Peter! I thought you didn't love me anymore," she confessed.

"What would you do if I didn't?" He wrapped his arms around her, resting his chin on her head.

"I don't know. Throw myself in the river or find another guy—one or the other."

"I'll never stop loving you, Marybeth."

And she believed

Down
By The
River

C.S. Adler

An Archway Paperback published by
POCKET BOOKS, a division of Simon & Schuster, Inc.
1230 Avenue of the Americas, New York, N.Y. 10020

ISBN: 0-671-45288-6

First Archway Paperback printing August, 1983

10 9 8 7 6 5 4 3 2 1

*For my mother-in-law, Erna Adler,
and my daughter-in-law, Fran Adler,
and for my father, with love.*

Chapter 1

She awoke to the moonlight. Something had fright-
ened her out of sleep but nothing seemed wrong. She
listened, but all she heard was the clock buzzing in
company with the insistent insect chorus outside the
screened window of their bedroom. The house creaked
as the light summer wind off the river played in the
attic. Still the fear coiled in her chest and her heart
beat too fast. He slept on peacefully beside her. She
stared at him, struck by the beauty of his hard mus-
cled, bare shoulders and back and the strong planes of
his face. He was so beautiful, sculptured by sleep, but
as unfamiliar as if he were a stranger. There, that was
it. The doubt tossed up from the depths of her dream
lay revealed like a beached whale on the surface of her
mind. What was she doing married to a stranger?

Cautiously she eased out of the double bed and
escaped to the chair beside the window. She settled
there with her arms around her nightgown-curtained
legs and her chin on her knees. She felt calmer away
from him. Black tree branches feathered in the wind
outside. The polished points of stars studded the inky
sky. She peered out toward where the river ran below
the bluff at the end of their yard. There it was, close as

1

*she had always longed to have it. Moonlight gilded the
river's black surface turning it into a mirror that
reflected the events of her life. It was as if the river
recorded her life, as if it carried the disappointments
and the pleasure and the meaning of it all in its
passage.*

The first time she ever saw Peter was in sixth grade.
She was too busy reading the note passed under the
desk to her from her friend, Reenie, to notice his
entry. But when the teacher introduced him to the
class, Marybeth looked up. She saw a boy with hair
the color of maple syrup, long eyelashes, and wounded
eyes that made her want to reach out and say, "Don't
be scared; you won't be alone here." He would need
support from someone in that class if he were as
puppy-soft as he looked. The class was dominated by a
trio of mean kids who kept the rest ducking for cover.
Marybeth assumed the trio were to blame when Peter
burst into tears in the middle of math later that morning. She knew the tears would make him an untouch-
able among the boys, and sure enough at lunch, he sat
alone at an empty table in the cafeteria. She couldn't
stand it. Even though her girlfriends thought she was
acting weird, she left the warm, feathered shelter of
her own friendly circle and asked Peter if she could sit
with him. He only hesitated a second before saying,
"Sure."

"Have they been bothering you?" Marybeth asked,
gesturing at the table of bullies.

"Who? Them? No," he said. "I just cry a lot lately.
I can't help it."

"They'll call you a crybaby," Marybeth warned
him.

"I know." He shrugged. "But I don't even know
when I'm going to start bawling. It just comes."

"Have you always been that way?"

"No. Only since my mother left."

"Oh!" she said with as much feeling as if it were her own hurt.

She knew that they would be friends when she discovered him waiting for Bus 54, her bus. They had the longest bus ride, more than an hour to the bluff over the river which was the raggedy edge of otherwise sleek, well-cared-for neighborhoods, the farthest outpost of the school district. She saw it as an omen that he had come to the bluff. Nobody else near her age lived there except for her sister Lily, and Lily was only eight. He was the friend she had been praying for. He was Marybeth's reward for helping Mama and trying to be cheerful even when it was hard to be and the temptation to feel sorry for herself was strong.

"Which is your house?" she asked him when the bus left them standing side by side on the empty highway on the far side of the bridge.

"That one." He gestured at the three-story-high Victorian house capped with layers of peaked roofs. It stood grandly back from the highway with its rear end to the match box cottages lined up along the bluff.

"You live with the Josselyns?" she asked in surprise.

"They're my grandparents."

"Oh."

"Why? Is something wrong with them?"

"No. They're sort of old though . . . and they don't talk much to anybody around here." And she hastened to excuse them. "It's probably because everybody on the bluff goes to that white little community church across from the fire house. Did you notice it at the crossroads there? And your grandparents go into town to church. That's all it is probably."

He didn't probe further. Instead he offered, "My

3

mother used to be a singer . . . Before she had me. That's why she dumped me on them . . . So she could be a singer again."

"Uh huh."

"But they're okay, I guess." He tipped his head toward the house. "They just don't say much."

"I'm sure they're nice," she said quickly, wondering how his father figured in, but not asking. "And anyway, you can always come over to my house whenever you feel like it. I'm just a few houses down—the one with the blue door and the hearts painted on the mailbox."

"I never made friends with a girl before."

"That's okay," she said. "I never made friends with a boy ever, so we're starting even." She grinned at him, coaxing a smile from him the way she did with Lily and her mother. It wasn't hard. His smile flashed as impulsively as his tears.

"Why don't you come on over later and meet my mother and sister," she said.

"Maybe," he said. "Maybe I will." He walked off with a jaunty stride that was purely male, nothing babyish in the way he walked. He was the cutest boy!

It pained her to watch them tease him in school, but she admired the way he took it. He ignored their name-calling and when they tripped him and sent him sprawling, he picked himself up coolly as if no damage had been done. If they challenged him to a fight, he fought back hard. He never called for help from any adult in authority, and he never told on anyone. They might have learned to respect him in time, but those sudden tear bursts of his continued to confuse them. His tormentors never understood that *they* weren't the cause of his tears.

Sometimes Marybeth passed the principal's office on her way to the bus after school and caught sight of him sitting on the bench in there, torn shirt and bruised face explaining his presence. Then she would wait outside the building until his detention was over and sit beside him on the late bus trying to talk him out of his depression. Sometimes when kids kicked Peter's books and papers around the floor of the classroom, Marybeth's friends would help her rescue his belongings. They were always quick to lend him pencils and paper or parts of their lunch when his got stolen. But his circle of girl protectors just made him more suspect in the eyes of the boys who should have been his friends. Marybeth saw it and grieved for him.

They were an oddity to their classmates, the only boy/girl pair in sixth grade. Gradually Marybeth's girlfriends drew away from her. She had little time in school to spend with them. At lunch she sat alone with Peter in an isolated corner of the cafeteria, and she had no way to see anyone except Peter after school. A couple of times she had accepted invitations to all-girl parties, but he had acted so unhappy at her temporary desertions that she gave up trying to maintain contact with her friends. "He's a spoiled brat," her mother said when Peter sulked and punished Marybeth with silence after a Saturday afternoon roller-skating party which she'd gone to without him. But Marybeth didn't blame him for his possessiveness. She knew he had no one but her, and she didn't consider the loss of her school friends too high a price to pay for his sake. Even in sixth grade Peter had begun to fill her world awake and dreaming as not even her beloved sister could do.

After the first time Peter met Lily, he had asked Marybeth what was wrong with her sister. "She's got cerebral palsy, but she's getting better all the time," Marybeth told him.

"Will she be cured soon?"

"Well, you don't get cured of it exactly, but Lily is lucky she doesn't have too bad a case. She can learn to control her muscles to walk and talk pretty near normal. Some people with C.P. are in wheel chairs and can't even lift a spoon to feed themselves."

"So is it like being retarded?"

"No, Peter. Nothing's wrong with her brain. She's smart, a lot smarter than me. It's just the part that controls her muscles that doesn't work right."

It annoyed Marybeth when anyone assumed Lily was retarded just because of her slurred speech and her lumbering walk. Even Doris, their mother, used to think Lily was retarded until Marybeth made her sister work so long on the tongue exercises the doctor gave her that Lily began speaking clearly enough for Doris to understand her. Doris had been pleased when she finally believed that Lily was mentally sharp, but even then she still treated her like a dependent baby.

"But Mama," Marybeth would protest. "If you don't expect her to do something, she's not going to learn to do it. It's awfully hard for her to do anything."

"Why make her try so hard then?" Doris asked. "You push her too much, Marybeth. You always make her cry. Leave her be."

"But Mama," Marybeth would insist, sure at the age of eight and nine and ten that she understood her sister's needs, that she was closer to Lily than Doris or anyone could be. "She needs to learn to do for herself. It's important."

"We can take care of her."

"But it's better for her to take care of herself."

Marybeth couldn't help judging people by how they treated her sister. She didn't want Lily treated as if she were less than human the way people tended to treat a handicapped person. So she watched Peter with Lily and was only satisfied when he began acting as if Lily

6

were any normal kid sister, which she was under the disguise of her unruly muscles and weak eyes. The yellow station wagon that took the handicapped students home would drop Lily off first. She would be waiting for them on the front steps when they came up the lane. Her puffy cheeks were round as her horn-rimmed glasses and magnified blue eyes, full as her smile of welcome.

"Did you have a good day? Did anything happen?" Lily would call, slurring the words together in her excitement so that only Marybeth could understand her.

"Guess what, Lily! Your sister kicked a home run for her team today," Peter would say, an outrageous lie to amuse her. "And you know what she did to me? She ate my ice cream at lunch when I wasn't looking."

"She didn't do that!" Lily would protest loyally.

"Oh yes, she did."

"You didn't do that, did you, Marybeth?"

"Don't believe a word he says," Marybeth said. "What really happened was I kicked a foul and Peter ate my ice cream when I wasn't looking."

"That sounds more like it," Lily agreed.

"How come you believe your sister and not me, Lily?" Peter would demand.

"Because my sister tells the truth and you don't."

"Boy, Lily, boy, you're mean to me," he'd tease. Then Lily's tissue-paper feelings would give way and the tears would fill her eyes.

"Now what did I say?" Peter would ask Marybeth. "What's she crying about now?"

"You said she was mean," Marybeth explained. "Lily's never mean."

"I didn't mean it, Lily. I didn't mean you were mean."

And eventually her smile would return, and Peter

would reluctantly go home to the dark rooms of his grandparents' house where the knickknacks of a lifetime received a daily dusting and a growing boy was also tended dutifully.

Two hours after he had left Marybeth, Peter would call her up and they would chat for half an hour: "What are you doing? . . . Nothing . . . That's what I'm doing too . . . They just played a new song on WMPS. You'll love it . . . How does it go? . . . Can't remember. I'll call you when it comes on again." Sometimes he called three and four times in one evening. She avoided calling him. His grandparents always wanted to know what she had to talk to him about. Then mostly they said he was busy and to see him in school about it tomorrow. They didn't approve of the friendship.

"They're snobs," Doris said.

"They're worried because Marybeth's a girl," Lily said.

Marybeth was more charitable. "It's just their way," she said.

Sometime in seventh grade kids stopped teasing Peter. The relationship between Marybeth and him was no longer an oddity but something the more socially mature kids envied. Peter and Marybeth were the first real couple their class had. While other kids made do alone or with a loosely tied group or glued to one friend, Peter and Marybeth had each other. Their individual weakness had somehow doubled into strength, and they walked under a halo of affection that was visible to everyone.

They were still walking hand in hand through the halls of the school in ninth grade, old timers among the ranks of the newly paired. Sometimes Peter would say, "When we're married . . ." but that was far off, comfortably far off beyond high school graduation.

"Don't you want to go out with other boys so you at least know what they're like?" Doris asked.

"What for?" Marybeth said. "Nobody could be better than Peter." She was completely happy.

He stirred in his sleep and turned toward her hugging the pillow to his chest. The stubble of his beard was spotlighted while the moon drew shadows around his eyes as if to warn her what he would look like when he was very old. He moved restlessly dreaming one of those unhappy dreams she had no part in. His arm crossed his eyes in self-protection, then lashed out. He groaned and turned again. She knew the bad dreams came out of his childhood, but he claimed not to remember them when he woke up, and he wouldn't talk about his past much. "No sense raking over old coals," he would say and set his mouth firmly in silence. Once he told her, "I don't want your sympathy, just that you keep on loving me."

She should fit her body back against his now. That would soothe him. She should be there beside him touching close. That was where he wanted her always, and she was his wife. She had promised to love, honor and cherish him, but she was too wide awake to lie down just yet. Too much moonlight remained on the river and so many memories waited for her there. She shivered slightly in the midnight air and tucked the nightgown under her toes and looked out again to where her life ran past in the flowing stream along with the answer to the question of how she had come to be here.

One hot summer night when she had just had her sixteenth birthday and Peter's was soon to come, Marybeth deliberately deceived her mother. Peter and she had planned it beforehand, how he would say goodnight and go home early. Then she would announce she was tired and go to sleep on the screened-in sun porch, where it was cooler than her bedroom, which got the sun all day. Then when Lily and Doris were asleep, he would come for her and take her down to see what the river was like at night.

"That's the first time I can remember him ever going home at a decent hour," Doris said. Peter's charm slid off her like so much rain off a slicker. Being deserted by her husband after Lily was born had left her immune to male charm. "What are you holding your hands like that for, Lily? You look like you're catching something."

"I am," Lily murmured dreamily.

"What?"

"Peter's kiss."

"Oh, my Lord! As if it isn't bad enough Marybeth's gone silly over that boy. Must you follow right after her?"

"Peter's my dream boy. Marybeth says I can have him for my dreams if I want."

"Marybeth!" Doris said sharply. "Why do you have to encourage such foolishness?"

"Dreams don't hurt, Mama."

"Who says they don't? That's the trouble with you. Too much dreaming and no reality. Listen, you're sixteen now. It's time you got your head screwed on straight. That boy only seems special to you because you haven't gone out with any others. It's not smart to put your eggs all in one basket."

"I don't see what you don't like about Peter, Mama."

"I don't dislike him. He's a nice enough boy, but he's just a *boy*, Marybeth, and I worry about how serious you are about him."

"I love him."

"So you say, and that's what worries me. Thinking you love him! You're gonna get carried away and go too far, and then you'll be in trouble."

"If Marybeth gets in trouble, Peter will marry her," Lily said.

"Oh, and I suppose you think it's great stuff getting married at sixteen? Well, believe me, it's not. The romance ends at the kitchen sink. I know. I've been there. You ruin your chance to make something out of your life when you rush into marriage too early. All that'll get you is stuck like me here by this river."

"Mama," Marybeth spoke into the tempest of her mother's fears. "I'm not going to get in any trouble. Peter and I don't do anything that would get me in trouble."

"Yet."

"Don't you trust me?"

"You're normal, and you love that boy, or think you do."

"Mama, can I tell you something?"

"What?"

"You won't get mad at me?" Marybeth's heart thumped wildly. She was finally going to say it. She was going to tell her mother. "If I ended up spending my life here on this bluff, I'd be happy. I like it here."

"I know that. I know you think that. It's because you're too young to know any better. That's all. Believe me, there's a whole lot more to life than what we've got here."

"We have each other. That's all I need, somebody to love who loves me back."

Inexplicably, Doris's eyes filled with tears and her anger disappeared. "Oh, Marybeth, you're such a fool," she said.

11

"Do you care if I sleep out on the sun porch tonight, Mama?" Marybeth asked on the tail of a convenient yawn.

"Go ahead. Sleep where you want. It's not going to be much cooler than your room though."

At midnight a strange-sounding owl hooted just outside the screen door of the sun porch. Marybeth sat up in bed and pulled on her jeans shorts over her underpants. She already had on a T-shirt. She whispered, "I'll be out in a second," as she felt for her sandals. She would have combed her hair for him, but he hissed impatiently.

"What's keeping you?"

She let her hair go and unhooked the latch on the door. "My, aren't we in a hurry," she teased him.

"You!" he said and clamped her against him to give her a kiss powerful enough to send her blood fizzing through her in a dizzy rush.

"So that's what you invited me out here for!" she said.

"It drives me crazy sitting there all evening without touching you, and your mother giving me those looks like I'm some kind of sex fiend or something. If I even hold your hand, she looks at me. Oh, Marybeth—" and his mouth drew slick, sweet, soft sensations in hers.

"She doesn't want anything bad to happen to me, that's all," Marybeth said when her lips were freed again.

"I think she hates me."

"Not you. She's just scared because you're so sexy, and she knows how I feel about you."

"How do you feel?"

"You know I love you, Peter." She pressed against him and kissed his eyes and nose and ears while their bodies tried to meld through their clothes, and she felt his hungering hard against her, and the moist, tingling center of her own body. She pushed him away.

"What are you afraid of?" he asked.

"You know."

"We could use something," he said huskily, "you or me."

"It's not just having a baby," she said. "There's more to it than that."

"What then?"

"Just something I feel, but I don't know how to say it . . . I want to wait."

"No, you don't," he said, touching her surely so that her body gave evidence that what he said was true.

"I can't, Peter. I don't want to hurt my mother, and we couldn't stop if we got started, and it's too long until we graduate. If we make love all those years, we won't have anything left when we get married."

"There'll be plenty left."

"But it won't be special."

"It's always special."

"I just want to wait."

"You said that before."

"I mean it."

"You're driving me crazy, Marybeth. I can't think about anything but sex. When I was sitting in class last year, that's all that was on my mind. It's no wonder my marks were lousy."

"Oh, blame me, why don't you!"

"Well, if you weren't such a tease—"

She pulled away from him in anger.

"Marybeth, baby," he said contritely. "I'm sorry."

"You're so unfair," she said. "You always make it me who has to hold back. You don't help, and you know I want you as much as you want me. Why don't you help me?"

"Because I don't see why we have to hold back. That's why."

"All right then." She sighed. "You were going to take me down the bluff so I could see how the river looks."

"Boy, you're something," he said. "Fight like a tiger about not making love, but too scared to climb around in the dark in a place where you've lived all your life."

"Aren't you scared of the dark a little?"

"No."

"Well, I am."

"Okay. Take my hand then. I'll protect you against all the wild beasts."

"You do that," she said refusing to be mocked. She took his hand, glad to let him lead her because she knew it made him proud to be the stronger in this way.

They crossed the lane and stole through the yard of the young couple who lived across from Marybeth. Frazier was their name. From the Fraziers' backyard, it was a steep climb down to the riverbank over tree roots bared by erosion, across crumbling ledges of rock and along the concrete wall that had lined the riverbank here before it broke up in the spring floods. They jumped down to the soft dirt of a gully where spring rain washed into the river and people had dumped rusted metal cans and bedsprings. The gully was dry now, and they could sit on a low branch of a bent tree overhanging the water and hear it lap against the rocky edge.

"Don't know what you expected to see, but here you are," he said.

"It's so mysterious at night," she said, awed by the dark body of water so alive in its continuous movement, yet so alien. The river made her feel as helpless as a wild wind or snowstorm did sometimes, but it fascinated her too. There was something, some secret wisdom, something—if only she listened hard enough to the silent, ceaseless, scurrying onward of the water as it passed the spindly houses on the bluff, flowed under the bridge where cars hissed by each other impatiently, and slipped by penny-sized islands marked by a single tree. If only she looked long enough into the glimmering mirror, if only she could become part of the meaning of it all. She shivered.

"Are you cold?" he asked.

"No."

"Yes, you are." He put his arms around her confidently and drew her into his warmth.

"How come you're always so warm?" She muffled her cold nose in the soft hollow of his neck. In the winter he went without gloves and wore his jacket open. While her pale skin got paler yet, his grew more ruddy.

"My hot blood I guess. Hey, Marybeth," he crooned.

"What?"

His hand slipped under the back of her shirt, and she shivered as his fingers stroked her. "I love touching your skin," he said. "There's nothing smoother. It's like—flower petals."

She smiled to herself and kissed him, but when his hands searched out her breasts she drew back. "Look out there," she said. "Something flashed in the water."

"Fish jump at night," he said, and released her. It was liquid quiet.

"But the water flashed like light. What does that?"

"How am I going to stay away from you for two whole weeks? I'm going to miss you too much."

"Don't talk about it, Peter."

"But we're leaving next Saturday."

"Then let's enjoy the time we have."

"How would you like to come with me when I go?"

"With your grandparents? They'd never let me come."

"But suppose they would. I could tell them I wouldn't go unless they invite you. They owe me. They wouldn't let me even look for a summer job, and Grandpa says no driver's license until I bring my grades up, but they can't just expect me to sit around doing nothing at my age."

"They'd probably let you bring a boy, Peter, but I'm a girl."

"I don't see what difference that makes."

She giggled. "You don't?"

"All right, I do, but . . . Listen, I'm going to ask them. You ask your mother."

"My mother probably wouldn't let me go anyway. Probably she'd worry."

"I can tell her there isn't a thing to worry about. You won't even let me past first base. Why should she worry? You'd be chaperoned."

"But your grandparents. She doesn't know them. If they were like family friends, maybe."

"My grandparents are pillars of the community, respectable citizens."

"But they stay to themselves. They don't mix with the people on the bluff."

"They don't mix with anybody much. All they do is fuss with things. Grandpa's always working in the yard or on his cars, and Grandma's polishing up some corner of the house nobody ever looks in anyway. Then they've got a few old geezers from their church they see once a month, and Grandpa sits on some boards of things and that's it. It's like living in a museum. I get to wondering if I'm dead or alive sometimes."

16

"But they care about you."

"Only if I grow up to be chairman of the board of something for them to be proud of me for."

She touched his cheek and said consolingly, "I care about you."

"I know you do. I don't know what I'd do if I didn't have you, Marybeth—kill myself maybe."

"Peter, don't talk like that."

"Okay. Let's talk about how it would be to spend a couple of weeks together at the lake in New Hampshire. Wouldn't you like me to teach you how to sail, and we could go swimming together."

"You know I can't swim."

"How can you live by a river and not know how to swim?"

"Easy. The river's too polluted to swim in."

"But there're pools."

"Mama used to take us to Central Park Lake when we were little. Maybe a couple of times during the summer we'd go."

"Yeah, and?"

"And I paddled around but I never learned to swim."

"Okay, so I'll teach you. I'm a pretty good swimmer. They asked me to be on the swim team, you know. Only I'd have to spend my life practicing."

"You're good at everything." She ran her hand over the sparely cushioned, muscular body, such a perfect male body with flat stomach and slim legs and small, tight butt and chest and shoulders flaring from the waist in a wide *V*. He was much more beautiful than she was. Her hips and thighs were too big and her body too soft. Doris said Marybeth would get fat someday, probably after her first pregnancy. "You'd better learn to like celery, Marybeth," Doris had said.

"Peter, do you think I'm pretty?"

17

"Sure you're pretty. Every time I see you I want to touch you. You got skin like butter. It makes me want to eat you up." He growled and bit gently into her neck, his fingers roaming over the billowing softness of flesh below her waist. She gripped his hands by the wrists and stopped them.

"Did you write your mother?" she asked.

"What for?" His voice had hardened. "If she doesn't remember it's my birthday, what's the use? She hasn't come in over a year now. I don't need her anyway."

"But she always remembers your birthday. She does think about you."

"Yeah, whenever she hasn't got anything better to do. Last year I told her I wanted a Swiss army knife and she sent money. I don't need her money."

"Maybe your grandparents would give you money for a plane ticket and you could go visit your mother instead of going up to their camp with them."

"Marybeth, you keep thinking I've got a regular mother. I don't. She doesn't want anything to do with me, and I don't care anymore. I've stopped crying over her. I've gotten over it."

She heard the soreness in his voice and said nothing, letting his fingers explore her softness instead. That was the best way she knew to comfort him.

When a faintly pink glow touched the milky white above the dark wall of land on the far side of the river, Marybeth shook Peter, who was dozing in her arms. They climbed back up the hill through a cacophony of birdcalls. Red-winged blackbirds slid back and forth overhead from bush to bush. A crow's wings beat heavy on the transparent air, and from the topmost branch of a tree, the trilling of an invisible bird pierced the morning. It was the birds' world. Marybeth thrilled to it, but she was anxious too. If anyone spotted them sneaking home now, they would be sure to think she was no good. But she was good. She was very good and very strong to be able to hold back the gush of her own desires and Peter's as well. She was proud of how strong she was, and because she couldn't seek praise from anyone else, sometimes Sunday mornings in church she let God know how she was doing.

Marybeth liked going to church. It refreshed her spirit to be with a community of people all bent on spiritual cleansing of one kind or another. She didn't listen to much of the service. She found it too hard to believe in the fires of Hell the minister was always dwelling on, and most of what he said about sin and how evil they all were didn't feel true to her either. But she believed thoroughly in the power of love and how important it was to try to love others more than yourself. She believed that to be good was to love with all your might. Once in a moment of fancy she had imagined her ability to love as a muscle that she was developing, a muscle whose strength could heal others. Her feeling for Lily had a lot to do with her religious sense. The patience it took to teach Lily to walk and talk and dress herself and feed herself had come out of love and been renewed by Lily's returning adoration. Marybeth had a secret pride in her ability to love. She thought it might be greater than most people's, the thing that she excelled in, her one talent.

Chapter 2

Marybeth awoke late after creeping home at dawn. She could hear her mother talking in the kitchen and her Aunt Janet's shrill laugh. Janet visited them at least once a week. Four years younger than Doris, Janet was the baby sister who had succeeded in escaping from the bluff, and to Doris, she was everything a woman should be. Janet was an independent single woman who supported herself in style without needing a man for anything but to take her out to dinner or a movie once a week. "You could do a lot worse than to grow up to be like your aunt," Doris always told Marybeth, ignoring the fact that Marybeth and Janet were as alike as tennis shoes and high-heeled dancing slippers. Janet's presence kept Marybeth from rushing right in and pleading with her mother for permission to go away with Peter. Her mother was likely to say no in any case, but sure to refuse if Janet disapproved. Just thinking about being away with Peter for two weeks made Marybeth's heart somersault. She had to persuade her mother somehow.

She ambled into the kitchen barefoot in last night's shorts and T-shirt with her hair still uncombed and a smile of greeting for Janet. Janet stopped what she was saying long enough to eye Marybeth with disgust. Every wave of Janet's hair was fixed just as the hairdresser had set it. She wore a light summer dress that showed off her small waist, and high-heeled leather shoes to set off the small feet she claimed were too delicate to tolerate anything but the most expensive shoes. Lily once said Janet reminded her of the princess and the pea story. She had said it out loud in front of Janet who had, as usual, been too busy making some point of her own to pay attention.

"So I told him," Janet said, offering her cheek for Marybeth's kiss, "I said, I thought my experience ought to count more than her degree. I mean, what is she going to learn in college that would be practical in our business? 'Look,' I said, 'I know all those salesmen on a first name basis, and when they want something from the shop in a hurry, Janet's the one they come to.' Now that should count for something. You can't just walk into that with a Master's in Business Administration. You got to earn it with hard work and coming through when they need you. 'And believe me,' I said, 'I'm worth a lot more in other ways than a young kid like her still wet behind the ears.' I'll tell you, Doris, I was so mad that he'd think of promoting that kid that he doesn't even know over me that if he'd of looked at me crosseyed, I'd of told him where he could stick his job."

"You should of told him, Janet. With your looks and ability, you could walk out of that office and get a better job in a minute." Doris leaned over her coffee cup as absorbed in her sister's story as if it were happening to her. "So then what did he say?"

"He said, 'All right. Don't get your blood pressure up. You can have the job.'"

"You're kidding! You got another promotion already?" Doris clapped her hands in delight and gave Janet a kiss. "That's terrific. You're really something else!"

"Congratulations, Janet," Marybeth said. She yawned and poured herself a glass of frozen orange juice. It was 10:45. In less than an hour her mother would leave for work, and Janet might not go until then. Marybeth had to know now if she had any reason to hope.

"Still tired, lazybones?" Janet said to her. "That must have been some date you had last night."

"I just sat around with Peter."

"That's all she ever does is sit around with Peter. You'd think she'd be tired of that kid after all these years," Doris said.

"It's nice to have a date you can depend on," Janet said, interpreting Marybeth to her mother and getting her all wrong as usual.

"Not having a date doesn't bother me," Marybeth said. "I can be happy just sitting home with Lily and Mama."

"Can you? Not me," Janet said. "If Saturday night comes and Stuart or somebody isn't taking me out, it gets me down. I don't know what I'm going to do when I'm over the hill."

"You'll never be," Doris said. "Look at you. You don't look a day over twenty. Not like me. I look more like forty than thirty-four."

"You look fine, Mama," Marybeth said giving her chunky, frizzy-haired mother an encouraging hug.

"Marybeth, why must you go around looking like such a slob?" Doris complained, taking the hug for granted. "Isn't that the same outfit you had on yesterday?"

"I'm going to take a bath and get dressed now."

"Well, don't sit in the tub for an hour like you usually do. I made a list of things I want done while I'm at work today."

"Sure, Mama. Want me to pour you another cup of coffee?"

"Thanks. Maybe Janet will try one of those chewy cookies you made yesterday. They're really good, Janet."

"None for me, thank you," Janet said. She rarely ate sweets and claimed to live on salads and fruits to keep her size ten figure. "Like a monkey," Lily had said. Lily liked Janet even less than Marybeth did. When Janet was around, Lily usually got one of her headaches and disappeared into her room to play her guitar and sing to herself.

"So," Janet said, eager to bring the conversation back to her favorite subject. "Guess what I went right out and did?"

"Bought yourself something new? A new pair of shoes, I bet!" Doris said.

Janet waved her foot in the air. "Would you believe these cost fifty dollars on sale? I said to the salesman, 'You just gotta be kidding. There's nothing to them. . . .' 'Miss,' he said, 'Miss, it's the last. Good shoes just have a different last to them.' "

Doris groaned. "Maybe I should get myself a pair of good shoes. Orthopedic shoes is what I need."

"Did you remember to wear your elastic stockings yesterday?" Marybeth asked.

"They don't help, honey. They really don't."

"It's that job. I told you before you ought to learn how to type so you could get yourself an office job," Janet said.

"Oh, it's not such a bad job," Doris spoke in the offhand way she used when one of them pushed her to change. "I'm so used to it anyways. I'll survive."

"You're hopeless," Janet said. "You act like you're an old lady. You're only thirty-four for God's sake!"

"Yeah, well, it's all in how old you feel."

"Are you staying for lunch, Janet?" Marybeth asked.

"No, honey. I'll leave when your mother goes . . . Want to hear about my latest fella, Doris?"

Doris beamed. "You know I do. Is this one serious?"

"Could be," Janet said.

"He's not—"

"Married? No, this time I know he isn't. The only thing is, I think he's a little on the cheap side."

Marybeth spread jelly on a piece of bread. Something was always wrong with Janet's men. If they weren't married, they had some problem that made them unmarriageable. Doris often talked about the bad luck her sister had with men, but Lily, who could be very smart about people, said she thought Janet picked the kind of men she couldn't marry on purpose. "What would she do with all her shoes if she had to share her closet with a man?" Lily said, and Marybeth had laughed, because shoes probably did rate higher than a husband with Janet. Marybeth had no doubt Janet would say, "Don't let her go," about the vacation in New Hampshire. How was she going to get her mother alone this morning?

"I thought you were going to get dressed," Doris said, catching Marybeth eating jelly by the spoonful. "You're going to get fat that way."

"I'd like to ask you something before you go to work, Mama."

"What's that?"

"I'll take a bath, and then can I speak to you for a few minutes?" She meant alone.

"Tell me now while I'm sitting here, not while I'm walking out the door. What's wrong?"

To erase the instant anxiety in her mother's voice,

Marybeth blurted out her question. "Nothing's wrong, Mama. Peter's invited me to go to his grandparents' camp with him for vacation."

"Did the Josselyns invite you, or just Peter?"

"Well, I told him I had to ask you first. But if they invite me, would you let me go?"

"Where is the camp?"

"In New Hampshire someplace. I've never been to New Hampshire."

"You've never been anyplace," Doris said. "We can't afford vacations on what I make. And for how long would you go?"

"I don't know, a week or two."

"Who would be there besides you?"

"I don't know, Mama. Probably just Peter and me and the Josselyns."

"Those old fogies that live in the big house off the highway?" Janet asked. "If you let her go with them, you're crazy, Doris. She'll come back pregnant for sure. They'll never be up to chaperoning two teenage kids."

"Peter and I can get in just as much trouble here as we could in New Hampshire," Marybeth pointed out.

"Yeah? How? There's eyes all over this bluff. You can't put a toe outside without half the neighborhood knowing," Janet said.

"It's nice," Marybeth said, "to live where people care what's happening to you."

"She's right, Janet," Doris said. "I couldn't go off and leave the girls alone here when I work nights if I didn't know the neighbors keep tabs on what's going on around the bluff. Everybody's friendly—except the two across the street, the Fraziers. They're as bad as the Josselyns. They won't have anything to do with the rest of us."

"Didn't Mr. Frazier fix your car when it wouldn't

start?" Marybeth asked. "He doesn't smile much, but he's nice when I babysit for them."

"And I suppose she's a sweetheart too?" Doris said, and to Janet, "Didn't even thank me when I brought over a cake when they moved in."

"She's not too friendly," Marybeth agreed.

"Well, I'm glad you're not such a goody-goody that you like everybody," Janet said. "I guess Marybeth's right though. If she's going to get in trouble, she will wherever she is."

"Marybeth's not going to get in trouble," Doris said fiercely. "She knows better than to end up like me. At least she should know better. I've told her often enough. She should go to college—at least community college—and get herself a decent job sitting down at a desk."

"Like your little sister?" Janet asked.

"She could do worse than be like you."

Janet stood up smoothing her dress down over her hips. "I guess I've done okay for myself," she said.

"I'll say you have! And all on your own, too."

Janet smiled. "No wonder I love coming here, Doris. You always make me feel good." The two sisters hugged and touched cheeks.

"You were always something special even when you were a little kid." Doris's voice was husky with emotion.

"So can I go if they ask me?" Marybeth interrupted them.

"Yeah, sure. If they ask you, why not?" Doris flipped out the permission as casually as if it were nothing, surprising Marybeth with her unconcern. "I better get my butt in gear or I'm going to be late for the lunch crowd. What are you up to today, Janet?"

"My usual. There's a sale on in jewelry at Wiggy's. Want me to see if I find something nice for you,

26

Marybeth? You could do with a new pair of earrings instead of those junky little blue flowers you wear all the time."

Marybeth's fingers flew to her ears and she said indignantly, "These are not junky."

"Peter gave her those for her birthday," Doris said, bringing her cup and saucer to the sink.

"Oh? He didn't strain his wallet any, did he?"

"These were the earrings I liked. They're forget-me-nots. I think they're pretty," Marybeth said.

"They match her eyes, Janet," Doris said, defending Marybeth.

"Well, she could use another pair anyways. I'll pick up something for Lily too, and what would you like, Doris?"

"Don't waste your money on me. Nothing's gonna help an old bag like me."

"Mama!" Marybeth protested. She hated hearing her mother belittle herself as she often did when Janet was around. "You're a young woman. Why shouldn't you dress up and look good too?"

"Ah, honey," Doris said hugging Marybeth against her stocky body. "Don't get upset. It's not that I'm complaining or anything, but I want you to understand what happens to a person. Living the kind of life I live wears you out. Waitressing's made an old lady of me, that and trying to pay all the bills without any money. That's why I'm after you all the time. I'm so scared you're going to end up married too young and tied down with kids like me."

It made Marybeth miserable when her mother talked like this. Even though she'd had no say in being born, it was her birth and Lily's that had trapped her mother, kept her, as she put it, "stuck in the mud of the house I was born in." But besides the guilt, there was anger. Marybeth resented it when her mother put herself down as "just a river rat." All Marybeth ever wanted was here on the bluff—Peter and Lily and the river and babies to cuddle someday.

"Did she leave yet?" Lily poked her owlish face around the doorjamb to peer into Marybeth's room.

"She left. Mother's gone too—to work."

"Good. Then we have the house to ourselves. I like it when it's just you and me. Then nobody interrupts what I have to say to you."

"What all do you have to say?" Marybeth asked with a smile.

"Nothing, but I like to be listened to, and you're the only one who listens to me."

"Mama listens."

"No, she doesn't. She doesn't listen to you either. She only listens to Janet. She doesn't hear what anyone else thinks . . . Let's be happy today, Marybeth."

"Yes, let's."

"That's why I love you so much," Lily said. "You're the only one who knows how to be happy." She shuffled into the room, dragging her leg in a way that told Marybeth it was hurting her. Dressed in baggy shorts and the kind of loose man's shirt Lily preferred because she said it covered her best, she looked as stocky and square as Doris. Only her hair was long and fine like Marybeth's and she had creamy smooth skin like Marybeth's.

"What are we going to do?" Lily asked flopping down on Marybeth's bed.

"Want to help me dust the living room?"

"No."

"Well, you can watch me clean it then. You can play your guitar for me while I work."

"Oh, you know I'm going to help you dust, Marybeth. I'll dust all the low things. We can sing together while we work."

"All right, and if we get the cleaning done early, we can go for a walk."

"To see Peter?"

"No. Peter's going somewhere with his grandfather."

"Is he coming over here tonight then?"

"He better not be. I told him I have to babysit over at the Fraziers', and she doesn't let her babysitters have their boyfriends come along. He's mad about it too, but I can't help it. If I'm going to buy him that hat, I've got to earn the rest of the money fast. His birthday's Tuesday. Do you want to come with me tonight, Lily? She won't mind if my sister comes."

"I'll see."

"Oh? You going to be busy?" Marybeth was amused.

Lily shrugged. "I could have a date, you know."

"Sure you could," Marybeth agreed. She had undressed and now she took a quick shower and put on shorts and halter, both too worn through to wear outside. They sang together as they cleaned house, old songs their grandmother had sung to them like "Just a Song at Twilight" and "Down by the Riverside."

When the sun had yellowed into late afternoon, they escaped the overheated house to the bench swing in the shade of the big tree in their backyard. Marybeth pushed the swing back and forth with one toe. It creaked horribly, but they both loved the swing. Lily strummed a few chords on the guitar every so often.

"Maybe I'll be going to New Hampshire with Peter for vacation," Marybeth said dreamily. "Wouldn't that be something?" The idea was a bright happiness at the edge of her mind. Telling Lily about it made it seem more real, but Lily ducked her head to her guitar and said nothing.

"Lily, what's wrong?"

"You're going to leave me all alone here for weeks."

"What's the matter with you? You're thirteen. That's old enough to stay alone. When you're thirteen you're old enough to babysit other kids. You're going to start menstruating pretty soon. You're practically a woman."

"I'm not going to menstruate."

"Of course you are."

"I'm not. I've got enough trouble already being C.P. I don't need that mess."

"Oh, Lily. Every girl menstruates sooner or later. It's just part of being a woman."

"I don't want to be a woman then."

"Don't you want to have babies?" Lily loved babies almost as much as Marybeth did.

"No. I'll play with yours."

"You're being silly," Marybeth said, but gently so as not to make Lily cry.

"I don't care. I can be silly if I want. You'll love me anyway."

"Mama and I both love you."

Lily considered. "In different ways though. Mama loves me, but she has to take care of me, and I'm hard to take care of and that wears her out."

"Nobody has to take care of you," Marybeth said firmly, sorry for Lily but knowing better than to show it. "There isn't anything you can't do for yourself, Lily."

"But I can't get a job. Nobody will hire me."

"You can give guitar lessons when you grow up."

"I don't want to. I'd rather sing for people."

"Well, maybe you'll do that," though her heart sank thinking of Lily's unpromising singing voice that was true but barely audible. "Anyway, there's going to be something you can do."

30

"Or I could come to live with you and Peter."

Marybeth laughed. "Peter doesn't need two wives."

"I could dust all your furniture for you and bake cookies," Lily wheedled.

"How about changing the babies' diapers?"

"No, you can do that."

"Some help you'll be!" Marybeth teased.

"Well, they'll be your babies," Lily pointed out.

"Anyway, Mama will be here with you if I go," Marybeth said, returning to the nub of the discussion.

"Not when she works."

"Don't you want me to go, Lily?"

"I want you to go, but I want you to stay home with me too."

Marybeth sighed. She understood perfectly what Lily meant. Often enough that was how it was with Peter too, where Marybeth had to want something that made his life better and hers worse. It wasn't easy to care more about another person than yourself.

Chapter 3

"I've got to see you tonight," Peter said into her ear as soon as she picked up the receiver. "I've gotta show you something. How about if I sneak over after the Fraziers leave?"

31

"No, Peter. You better not. I'm late now. I'll see you tomorrow."

"Marybeth, don't be so stubborn."

"Peter, it's just one night and I need the money."

"What for?"

"You'll see."

"You can't do this to me. It's Saturday night!"

"I'll see you after church tomorrow. Bye." She hung up and went running across the lane to the Fraziers' house. To her relief, Mr. Frazier answered the door. He looked so grim that she was a little afraid of him, but at least he answered questions. His wife acted as if any questions Marybeth asked were stupid, even about things as important as the children's bedtimes and what to feed them if they woke up hungry at night. Once Laura Frazier hadn't even told Marybeth that Lise was sick, and Marybeth had to sit and rock the sobbing child for hours without daring to give her any of the medicine she saw standing on the kitchen counter just because Laura hadn't bothered to leave any instructions about it.

Tonight Marybeth asked quickly, "Mr. Frazier, would you please leave a number where I can reach you in case of emergency?"

He flipped his blond hair out of his deep, brown eyes revealing the thick, dark eyebrows that were angled like a bird's wings in flight and were just as beautiful, Marybeth thought. "We're going bowling, the Empire Bowling Alley."

"Oh. Okay. Do you think you'll be back late?"

"Midnight maybe. It better not be later than that. I've got to overhaul a transmission for somebody tomorrow."

"Tomorrow's Sunday."

The corners of his mouth lifted slightly. "Do you think I'll go to Hell for working on Sunday?"

Just last week that was what the minister had said. "God wouldn't send you to Hell for anything that small," Marybeth said confidently.

"He wouldn't?" The brown eyes warmed in the crinkles of a smile. "You think our minister's got Him wrong then?"

"I hope so." Marybeth smiled back.

"I hope so too," Mr. Frazier said, but his smile faded as he turned at the sound of footsteps. Laura Frazier was coming down the stairs looking gorgeous in well-fitting pants and a silky green blouse that matched her cat's eyes.

"Wow, do you look pretty!" Marybeth said in admiration.

Laura barely glanced at her. Her eyes fixed on her husband. "Are we going or not?" she asked.

"I'm ready."

"Are the kids in bed yet?" Marybeth asked.

Laura looked at her briefly. "No, they're watching TV."

It was eight o'clock. "I guess I'll start them off to bed then," Marybeth said. "Do you want me to give them baths?"

Laura shrugged. "Whatever turns you on. But keep them up as late as you can, huh? Maybe they'll sleep tomorrow morning instead of getting me up at dawn."

"Right," he said. "Wouldn't want you losing your beauty sleep over your kids, would we?"

Marybeth looked at him to see if the bitterness she thought she heard in his voice was written on his face. It was. They'd had a fight over the kids she guessed. "Well, have a nice time and don't worry about a thing," she said cheerfully. She left them to say whatever they had to say to each other and made haste up the bare wood staircase to the kids' bedroom. It had an accordion-style gate across the doorway to lock them in. The bedroom held a crib with sides down for two-year-old Eric and a twin bed for four-year-old Lise, plus a linoleum-covered floor buried under plastic toys and metal trucks and stuffed animals. The children were watching a small TV on a shelf on the wall.

"Marybeth!" Lise screamed gleefully and deserted the TV to fling herself into Marybeth's arms. She curled her twiggy legs around Marybeth's waist and squealed in delight as Marybeth twirled her around. Eric yanked at Marybeth's pants. "Me too, me too!" She gave them swinging rides and lots of hugs and kisses before carrying them both off to the bathtub, which was afloat with plastic ducks and boats to amuse them.

The five red marks on Lise's back made Marybeth wince. "Did someone hit you, Lise?"

"Mommy hit me. I was bad."

"What did you do?"

"I don't remember." Lise's eyes clouded and she looked away from Marybeth. Next she grabbed a rubber tugboat from Eric who immediately howled. Lise didn't want to talk about it, Marybeth thought. As she gently toweled Lise dry, she saw the bruise behind the child's ear. She didn't ask about it though. Instead she decided she would watch the children, and if she saw anymore, she would go tell the minister. He would know what to do. Laura never went to church, but she had had the children christened there.

Marybeth couldn't find any books to read aloud, so she told them the story of Peter Rabbit. They fell asleep quickly. Each angelic face got one last kiss before Marybeth wandered downstairs and into the kitchen. From the window over the sink, she could see the river. The Fraziers were lucky to have a view of the river and lucky to have such cute little kids. What was wrong with Laura? Her children were sweet and obedient, so much fun that Marybeth and Lily sometimes came over just to play with them. Though when they did, Laura was likely to trap them into babysitting for free longer than they wanted to stay. "If you're going to be around anyway, I think I'll take a nap," she would say and disappear for hours. Marybeth didn't really mind, but it did seem to her that Laura needed an awful lot of sleep for a healthy-looking twenty-one-year-old woman. Such a beautiful woman with masses of wavy, brown hair and those slanty green eyes, but she had a remote look about her, as if she wasn't there in her skin. Maybe Mr. Frazier was mean to her and that was why she was unhappy. Anyway, Laura wasn't any business of Marybeth's, but if the kids were being abused, she certainly would make them her business.

Sunday morning Marybeth was startled out of sleep. Something was exploding under her bedroom window. She stumbled to the window, still in her pajamas, and looked down fearfully. Peter on a motorcycle. From the window of the bedroom next to hers, Doris's sleep-torn face appeared surrounded by a snarl of hair.

"What's that racket down there?" Doris yelled.

Peter varoomed the motorcycle for answer, grinning up at them from the seat of the black metal beast bedecked with silver-spoked wheels and silver-colored armor. "Isn't she a beauty?" he asked.

"You're a raving maniac!" Doris said furiously, "waking me up in the middle of the night to show off a motorcycle. They ought to cart you off and lock you up. Get that noisy thing out of our yard this minute, or I'll call the police on you, you hear?"

"Mrs. Mason, can I wait till Marybeth comes down? I want to take her for a ride."

35

"On that thing? No way! Never. You want to kill her? And besides you're too young to have a license. You'll get in trouble."

"Not if I stay on the lane or around our house. It's okay if you don't use it on the road."

"Well, I don't care how you take yourself to Hell, but you're not taking my daughter with you. You don't even have a helmet for her."

"Yes, I do." Triumphantly he held up a white helmet that was strapped on behind his seat.

"Mama, I'll be all right. I'd just go for a ride. Peter will go slow for me."

"Motorcycles aren't made to go slow. All's I need is to have you break something. Then who's going to pay the doctor bills? You stay off that thing, Marybeth. You hear?" Doris slammed her window shut even though the morning air was dew-fresh and delicious.

"Marybeth, put something on and come down. You got to meet my honey baby in person. Isn't she fabulous?"

"It's beautiful, Peter," she said, indulging him even though the armored thing clashed horribly with the summer smells of grass and warm earth and the delicate, gauzy air. "Is it yours?"

"My birthday present from Grandpa."

"How come you got it already? Your birthday's not till Tuesday."

"I've got to tell you about that. I had to make a deal with him."

"I've got something to tell you too."

"Something good?"

"Very good," she said.

"Well, hurry up down. I'm getting a stiff neck looking up at you."

It took her seven minutes to brush her teeth, use the toilet, wash her face and hands, throw on some clothes, brush her hair and get downstairs. She couldn't wait to tell him that she could go to New Hampshire with him. She restrained her eagerness though to let him share his excitement first. Dutifully she admired the machine which he straddled while he extolled its wonders to her in a gibberish from which she understood only the words "twin cylinder" and "transmission ratio" and "tire treads." She waited patiently for her turn. Finally he said, "What's your good news, Marybeth?"

"Mama gave me permission to go."

"For a ride?"

"No, silly. To go to New Hampshire with you for vacation."

"Oh." He didn't sound pleased.

"Well, isn't that great?"

He caressed the grips on his handlebars without looking at her. "Thing is," he said, "the way I got the motorcycle was so I'd stop badgering Grandpa about taking you along to New Hampshire. I mean, I could tell they weren't going to give in about inviting you anyway, so I thought I might as well get *something* out of it at least." He looked at her directly, his long-lashed eyes full of apology. "Are you mad at me?"

She tasted the bitter bark of disappointment, swallowed finally and said, "No, I'm not mad. Only I was sort of looking forward to going."

"I'm awfully sorry, Marybeth. If it was up to me, you'd be going. You know that."

"It's okay. Don't feel bad about it. Did they say why they didn't want to take me along?"

"Same as your mother. They don't want to be responsible for you and me—for what we might do together. I told them you weren't that kind of girl, but I don't think they believed me."

She sighed. "Yeah, well, anyway, it's a nice bike."

She wondered if now her gift was going to be an anticlimax.

"Do you think we can talk your mother into letting you go for a ride?" Peter asked.

"I don't see how."

"You know what? I could take her for a ride first to show her how safe it is."

"She'd never get on."

"Wanna bet?"

He joined them at the breakfast table, accepting a cup of coffee that was half milk with three spoons of sugar and one of the leftover rolls from the diner where Doris worked. Lily was in one of her melancholy moods. She leaned against Peter's side, no doubt pretending that he was her boyfriend. Doris was hunched over her coffee looking as if she wanted to creep into the cup. She was wearing her torn-at-the-elbows blue flannel robe, which indicated that she was feeling low. What a dim Sunday morning, Marybeth thought, and wished she could go back to bed and try waking up again.

"Did you ever have a boyfriend who had a motorcycle, Mrs. Mason?" Peter asked. He was the only one there exuding vitality.

"Why?"

"Just interested."

"I went to school with a kid got himself killed on one," Doris said.

"You ever ride on one yourself though?"

"Once—maybe a few times."

"Did you like it?"

She frowned at him. "It was okay. I was too young to know any better."

"But it was fun, wasn't it?" Peter asked hopefully.

"I don't remember." But then she did remember; her smile gave her away. "That kid with the motorcycle, he was too much. He was the guy I was going with when I met Hank."

"Hank?" Peter asked.

"My father," Marybeth said.

"Some father!" Doris snorted. "I bet you don't even remember what he looked like. He left when you were no more than four years old—the deadbeat. You'd think I'd of had more brains than to pick a guy with no sense of responsibility—none at all. He could smile though—like you, Peter. He could light up the sky with his smile."

"But the guy with the motorcycle," Peter reminded her. "You were saying about him."

"Oh yeah. He was a real character—used to leave quarters stuck to the sidewalk with gum and then laugh like a maniac when people picked them up. And he fed his dog beer all the time—what he didn't drink himself—every night. I'm lucky I didn't fall for him. Probably I'd still be stuck with him. What a character!"

"I'll bet you haven't ridden a bike since then though," Peter said.

"No, can't say as I have." She looked at him suspiciously. "Not that I'm missing anything."

"Yeah, I guess when you get older there's a lot of stuff you don't feel like doing anymore."

The coffee cup clattered down. "Listen, how old are you making me out to be? I may look lousy, but I'm not over the hill yet."

"Well, but I mean you've gotta be really fit to ride a motorcycle. I mean, I can see where you'd be scared to get on one at your age."

"Listen, I could still ride a bike without falling off, believe me."

"You could? Why don't you show us then? One slow turn up the lane and back."

"You little con artist! What are you going to be like in a few years, Peter Josselyn, if you're such a little con artist now?"

"Mama!" Marybeth objected.

"Mama's right," Lily said, lifting herself off Peter's arm. "Peter's just trying to get her to let Marybeth go riding with him."

"How about you, Lily? You want to go for a ride with me?" Peter asked.

"Not me!" She shook her head emphatically. "I'd be scared."

"Mama, would you like me to make you some eggs?" Marybeth asked.

"No, thanks, honey. I'm going to eat a piece of that pie I brought home last night. Cut a piece for Peter too. Look, I'll tell you what. Marybeth can go for a ride around the lane if you swear on your word of honor that you won't go over ten miles an hour."

"Boy, Marybeth is lucky to have a mother like you!" Peter said. He hoisted himself across the table and kissed Doris on the cheek.

"Oh, stop bothering me now," she said. "I don't know how I let you talk me into this. I probably should have my head examined. Come on, Marybeth, we got to hurry and get dressed for church."

The motorcycle ride was tolerable after lunch when it finally took place. Marybeth rested her head against Peter's back, closed her eyes and held on to him tightly until the roaring and bumping had stopped. To his eager question, "How did you like it?" she answered, "I liked it fine." But the bitter bark taste remained in her mouth all day, and it was hard to play back his enthusiasm to him.

Monday was Doris's day off. She took Marybeth and Lily to the mall and set them loose to shop while she ambled through the stores checking out fall clothes for teenagers to make sure what she sewed for her girls would be in style. Marybeth skittered off with Lily, sandals slapping the tiled corridor to the mini mall. The leather boutique there had the cowboy hat Peter had admired. The hat was real leather with a peacock feather band around its curled-up brim. Peter had looked like a movie star in it.

"Oh wow!" Lily said when she saw it in the window. Her mouth opened round as her glasses. "Marybeth, can you really afford that?"

"I've been saving all summer."

"Did you tell Mama?"

"About the hat? No. Why should I have?"

"How much does it cost?"

"Fifty dollars."

Lily tried to whistle.

"But it's what he wants, Lily. A birthday present should be something you really want, shouldn't it?"

"Suppose I wanted something that expensive. Would you get it for me?"

Marybeth considered. "Well," she said, "I'd try. But you better not work up any really expensive wants in a hurry, Lily. I'm going to be flat broke after this."

Lily squeezed her hand. "I'm glad you're buying the hat for Peter. I think it's beautiful," she said.

Marybeth was pleased. Lily always did understand.

In her own estimation, Marybeth was dressed up for shopping in her scoop-neck T-shirt, wrap skirt and sandals, but the salesman, who was lean and wearing clothes that looked as if they were pasted on his body, looked at her with a disdain that made her feel shabby. When he looked at Lily the same way, Marybeth got angry.

"I'd like to see that hat in the window," she said boldly.

41

"Sorry. I can't take it out. It's part of the display."

"Last time I was in here the salesman took it out."

"Sorry."

"I want to buy it for my boyfriend's birthday."

"It's a very expensive hat."

"I know that."

He frowned at Marybeth doubtfully. "You have the money with you?"

"Show him the money, Marybeth," Lily whispered. The salesman had cowed her utterly.

"I can pay for it," Marybeth said, "but first I want to check it over—if you don't mind."

Reluctantly the salesman leaned over the partition at the back of the display window and lifted out the hat. Marybeth took it lightly into her hands and turned it round and round.

"Careful," he said. "Leather gets sweat stained easily."

Marybeth turned around defiantly and set the hat on Lily's sweaty brow. "Look in the mirror, Lily, and see how you look in it," Marybeth ordered.

Lily smiled and shuffled over to the full-length mirror near the rack of leather jackets. She put her hands on her broad hips and swaggered in front of the mirror. "Howdy, pardner!"

"Can you wrap it up nice?" Marybeth asked the salesman.

"Sorry. I can put some tissue paper over it and put it in a bag, but we don't have a box that would fit that hat."

Marybeth considered. It seemed unfair to pay so much for a gift and not even get fancy wrapping for free, but then, Peter was going to be happy with the hat, not the gift wrap. "Okay," she said, and took out the old, blue leather wallet Janet had given her for

Christmas years ago. She had the fifty dollars in her hand when the salesman finished writing the sales slip. "Here's the money," she said.

"It's fifty-two dollars," he said. "There's tax, you know."

She stared at him wide-eyed and faltered for the first time. "I don't have more than the fifty."

He looked at her without expression. "I've got to charge you the tax."

"But—" Marybeth protested, "but—"

"You could find Mama and ask her to lend you two dollars," Lily whispered.

Marybeth shook her head. "No, that wouldn't be right."

"Guess your boyfriend wasn't supposed to get the hat after all," the salesman said with cheerful malice.

Lily tugged at her arm. "I'll lend you two dollars," she said. Marybeth looked at her. Lily was notoriously stingy. She claimed it was because she got such a little allowance and there were so many things she wanted, but Doris said Lily was just plain cheap. It was a family joke which always provoked Lily to complain that it wasn't her fault she had no way of earning money. Nobody ever asked her to babysit or pick berries the way Marybeth did sometimes, and Doris didn't give Lily much allowance unless she happened to get an especially big tip. But there was Lily dumping out her change purse on the counter and carefully counting out two dollars in quarters, nickels and dimes.

"There," Lily said. "Maybe you could find a box if you looked real hard. After all, a fifty-two-dollar present shouldn't just come wrapped in tissue paper."

The salesman looked her in the eye and wilted. "I'll see what I've got that might fit," he said, and departed for the back room.

Marybeth looked at Lily with respect. "You really are something!" she said.

"I don't know why you have to give him such a nice present when he isn't even making his grandparents take you to New Hampshire," Lily grumbled.

"He couldn't make them."

"Oh, sure he could of. He made Mama change her mind, didn't he?"

"Mama's easier than his grandparents."

"No, she's not. He just wanted the motorcycle more."

"Lily, that's a mean thing to say!"

"Well, but it's true though."

"Suppose it is? I don't care. I love him anyway, and I don't want to hear you saying any more nasty things against him."

"I gave you the two dollars, didn't I?"

"Oh, big deal! You know you'll get it back." Marybeth was angry, more angry with Lily than she had ever been in her life. Now she looked at Lily's shocked expression and saw tears flood her eyes and overflow. All of a sudden Marybeth felt awful. She put her arms around her sister, who hugged her back. The salesman, returning with the hat in a big cardboard box, stared at them as if they were the strangest pair he had ever seen.

Tuesday morning Peter came over as soon as he got up, just as Marybeth had requested. Marybeth said, "Happy sixteenth birthday, Peter," and gave him the hat. His delight was all she had hoped. He made almost as much fuss over the hat as he had over his motorcycle, and even though the temperature was in the nineties for a whole week of heat wave, and the hat must have weighted down his head, he wore it every day. Lily had told Marybeth she was sorry she had said anything mean about Peter, and Marybeth had apologized for being nasty to Lily. It was the first time either of them could remember Marybeth ever being nasty. Together they had baked a chocolate cake with vanilla icing for Peter's birthday. So everything should have been fine, but Marybeth kept slipping into a sadness she couldn't shake. Saturday Peter would leave. She wouldn't see him for two whole weeks. For her, that took most of the pleasure out of what remained of the summer.

"Are you going to miss me?" he asked her the evening before he had to leave.

"Oh, once in a while maybe I will," she said lightly.

"I'll expect a letter every day." He took her hands and kissed her knuckles one at a time. They were in the swing, creaking gently back and forth under a moon that lit up the night like a streetlamp, but the whispering foliage of the tree above them screened them partially from the house.

"I'll write you," Marybeth said. "But this year you better write me back."

"I wrote you last summer."

"Two postcards don't count."

"It was more than two."

"Well, the third one didn't come till after you got home."

"You know how I hate to write letters, Marybeth. It isn't anything for you, but for me writing's hard. I can think of what to say if I'm talking, but I can't get it down on paper. I guess I'm really sort of dumb."

"You're not. You're the sweetest, kindest, handsomest, cutest, nicest boy in the world, and you're as smart as you need to be."

"You like me, huh?"

"Pretty much. How do you feel about me?"

"Really want to know?"

45

"Really."

"I love you, Marybeth."

"A lot?"

"Enough so I'm going to miss you probably more than you'll miss me. You're the one makes me feel like I'm somebody special. Grandpa treats me like a dog he's got to housebreak, and Grandma treats me like a baby she wishes she didn't have to take care of. I'll tell you, school doesn't make me feel too hot either—all those D's and C's."

"That's not because you're not smart. It's just you don't try hard enough."

"That's what Grandpa says. I don't know. I do okay in things like shop and small engines. I did great in woodworking last year. What would you think if I become a carpenter after high school?"

"Sure, if that's what you want to do."

"Grandpa would hate it though. He says I've gotta go to college. He says if I don't start bringing my grades up, he's going to get me a tutor so I can get into college. He's got a real thing about college, and you know why?"

"Why?"

"Because he says if I don't go, I'll end up stuck here by the river all my life."

"What's so bad about that?"

"Well, I don't really think I'd like living here forever, Marybeth. I mean, that'd be pretty boring."

"Would it?"

"Sure. Maybe you don't think so because you've never been anywhere, but believe me, there's a million places more exciting than here."

"Maybe there are more exciting places, but it's peaceful here and small and the river's here. Don't you love the river?" she asked.

The arm that lay lightly around her shoulders tight-

46

ened. She let him pull her around so that her lips met his in a long, searching kiss. With her eyes closed, she felt as if she were weightless in a soft, slick tunnel. When the kiss fell away, he whispered. "I wish you were coming with me tomorrow. I really wish you were. You know what I'm going to have to do? I'm going to have to take my hat with me so I have part of you along."

To keep the gray fog of misery that the thought of being without him brought from closing in on her, she let his hands slip under her shirt and up to the tenderness of her breasts. His fingers circled like moths around a flame. "Let me kiss you there," he begged.

"No!" she gasped. "No, we better go in." But his teasing fingers sent electric shocks through her, and she needed to feel his mouth sucking wetly on her pulsing nipples. It was impossibly hard to keep saying no when her body felt so weak, and he was going away tomorrow and she wanted him so much.

"Marybeth!" Her mother's voice from the house froze his fingers. "You and Peter come in now and have some Coke with us."

"Do we have to?" he asked, his fingers pressing lightly.

"Yes," she said, pulling away from him. "Yes, we do." She stood up, glad her mother had called just then. Her body was so weak with desire she could barely hold herself upright.

Chapter 4

Early-morning sun shone in her eyes when Marybeth awoke. The room was already too warm. She felt mud heavy and then remembered why. Peter was gone. Immediately, she made herself start thinking of what she would do that day. Weed the little vegetable patch she and Lily had planted hopefully in the sunny back corner of the yard. They always planted a vegetable patch, and they always let the weeds take it over as soon as it got hot. There were still some carrots and eggplants that might grow if she gave them elbow room. Later in the day, she and Lily might go over to play with the Frazier kids. She heard the phone ring, rolled out of bed and padded downstairs to answer it.

"Marybeth? This is Garth Frazier. Could you come take care of my kids today?"

"Sure," she said, puzzled, because usually it was Laura who called. "When do you want me?"

"As soon as you can get here. I'll need you to stay until I get home from work tonight. Unless. . . .Can you do that?"

"Sure. Why not? I'll just leave a note for my sister to let her know where I am, and I'll be right over." It was too hot to weed the vegetable garden anyway. Marybeth yawned and poured herself some juice.

Then the undertone of urgency in Mr. Frazier's voice echoed back to her and she began speeding up her movements.

Twenty minutes after the phone call, she knocked on the Fraziers' kitchen door. Inside the kitchen, she could see Mr. Frazier feeding Eric, who was in his high chair while Lise sat at the table, her nose barely above the level of the bowl of cereal she was eating.

"Door's open," Mr. Frazier said. He glanced at her, unsmiling. "That was fast."

Lise yelled, "Hi, Marybeth," and deserted her cereal to run over and give Marybeth a kiss. Eric chortled enthusiastically, "Hi, hi, hi." He slapped his feeding table with his hands so hard the cereal bowl jumped and spattered wet globs all over his face and his father's shirt. Eric looked up at his father in open-mouthed surprise. Marybeth laughed. When his father smiled, Eric decided he'd done something great, so he slapped the table again.

"Hey, you monster, stop that!" Mr. Frazier said. He went to the sink to wash himself off while Marybeth wet a paper towel and went to work on Eric.

"Any instructions?" Marybeth asked while she kissed Eric's now clean face and fed him some more cereal.

"No. Just hold the fort till I get home tonight . . . unless my wife calls. Or if she should come back. You could give me a call at the garage if she comes back. I'll leave my number."

The uncertainty in his voice meant wherever Laura had gone, she had left unexpectedly. "It's all right if I fill the pool, isn't it?" Marybeth thought to ask.

"Yes. Listen, if—if it should turn out that she's gone for a few days, if I need you—"

"Is she all right? Was there an emergency or something?" Marybeth asked.

49

"No emergency," he said, and his lips closed firmly. He didn't want to talk about it.

"Well, I'm available all week if you need me," Marybeth hastened to say. "I don't have any big plans that can't be changed."

"I hope it's not all week. I don't know as I could pay you for that many days."

"Oh, don't worry about that. If you need me here you don't have to pay me. After all, we're neighbors, aren't we?" She put as much cheerfulness as she could into her voice to make him feel better, but to her amazement her words, or whatever was on his mind, brought a twitch to his jaw and a sudden gloss to the brown eyes under the dark, swallow-winged eyebrows.

"I couldn't let you stay for nothing. But I might have to owe you," he said. "Things are sort of in a mess. I—"

"Don't worry, Mr. Frazier. Really. Remember when Mother's car gave her all that trouble last winter? I don't remember you sending us a bill for what you did for us."

He shook his head wordlessly at her. She's run away from him, Marybeth thought. Why? But Laura couldn't have run away and left the children. No mother would walk out on her children like that, certainly not kids as adorable as these were. She looked down at Lise, who was plucking at her shorts, and thought of Peter, whose mother had left her husband and then left her son. Some people were beyond her understanding.

"Read me the funny book you brought us, Marybeth. Read me the funny book, please."

"Sure, Lise, if you help me clean up the breakfast dishes first."

"Can I wash?"

"Sure you can wash. I'll fill the dishpan and put the soap and dishes in for you. Okay?"

"Oh goody! I love washing dishes and Mommy never lets me."

Marybeth grinned at Mr. Frazier, inviting him to share her amusement at an innocence that could find entertainment in dishwashing, but he was staring at her with the strangest look. "You like children, don't you?" he said.

"Me?" Marybeth said. "I love kids. Mother used to say I ought to be a nursery-school teacher, but for that you need four years of college, and they say there aren't too many jobs available working with little kids anyway. I guess everybody wants that kind of job if they can get it."

"Not everybody," he said, and then, "I'm late for work. I better get with it."

Marybeth watched him stride out the back door. He was so tense, charged full of things he didn't want to express, that she was glad to see him go. Now she had the children and the house all to herself. She liked that. She filled the dishpan with soapy water and carried the rest of the dishes to the sink, moving a chair over so Lise could stand on it and play at dishwashing for half an hour. Some spoons and a cup with a few raisins served to keep Eric occupied. The river was gleaming with sunlight under the bluest of skies. On the far side a skinny tree, precariously rooted high in the narrow ribs of rock ledge, seemed poised in diving position above a passing yacht. A motorboat sped nose-up on the placid surface leaving its outsized vee-shaped wake to sign its passage. Even the auto repair shop that had a ramshackle dock on the river bank below its car-littered backyard reflected the sunlight in cheerful glints from its myriad glass and metallic surfaces. Marybeth was so content that she almost forgot Peter's absence.

When Mr. Frazier got back home that evening at seven, Lise and Eric were bathed and in their pajamas. Seeing the pizza box in his hands, Marybeth said, "The kids have already had supper. I left some salad stuff and sausage for you. Maybe you could freeze the pizza."

"You didn't have to feed them. Where did you get the food? There's nothing in the refrigerator."

"Don't worry about it. Food's one thing we always have plenty of. Mother brings home lots of stuff from the restaurant. The cooks there like her. It's still good stuff even if it's leftovers. You wouldn't believe what people throw away in restaurants. The waste is really awful."

He considered for a minute in silence. Marybeth couldn't imagine what was still bothering him. She tried, "The pizza will freeze perfectly well. We've done it before."

"It's not the pizza," he said. "I'm just not used to people doing things for me. Thanks, Marybeth. . . . Listen, you've had a long day. You must be anxious to get out of here." He dug his wallet out of his back pocket and withdrew some bills. Then he frowned and asked quickly, "She didn't call, did she?"

"Mrs. Frazier? No."

He bent his head and muttered, "I may be needing you again tomorrow."

"Good. I enjoyed myself a lot today. Your kids are so good. They're a pleasure to take care of." She was working hard to cheer him up, but he looked at her directly and again there was the gloss of tears. Why, he's handsome, she thought, seeing him suddenly as a male, rather than as the married man who lived across the street. He was just as handsome as Laura was pretty. What a shame two such beautiful people should be having trouble with each other. She knew by then that Laura had left him. She knew because Lise had hidden in her mother's closet playing hide-and-seek, and when Marybeth found her there, Lise had said,

"Mommy put all her clothes in boxes and she went away in a taxi. Where did she go, Marybeth?"

"I don't know, honey."

"Is she coming back soon?"

"I hope so."

"Who's going to take care of us when she isn't here?"

"Your daddy will."

"And you?"

"And me, for a while."

"I love you, Marybeth."

"I love you too, punkin." And Marybeth went another round of hugs and kisses, light as butterfly wings and gentle as summer.

She strolled home wishing Peter were there to share the velvet evening with her. Summer-soft evenings were always twice as lovely shared. The house was dark and hot, but the flickering white of the TV set shone in the living room, where Lily and Doris sat watching a show while a fan blew air at them and they emptied a bag of potato chips between them.

"Any news over there, Marybeth?" Doris asked. "Did she get in touch with him at least?" Her bare feet were propped on a hassock. Her feet always hurt, even though today she had worked the breakfast and lunch combination, which she said was easier for her than dinner. The dinner shift got her home near midnight, but usually meant bigger tips.

"I don't know, Mama. I don't think she did though, because he asked me if Laura had called."

"Well, I'm not surprised. I could have told you when I first saw that girl it wouldn't last. She didn't look like the kind who'd settle for being a river rat. Why should a girl that pretty spend her life drowning in bills and dirty diapers? Probably she only married him in the first place because he knocked her up."

"Mama, don't talk like that. You don't know why they got married. Maybe they just fell in love and decided they couldn't live without each other."

"No. She thought too much of herself to marry a grease monkey like him who's never going to have an extra dollar in his pocket. He must have gotten her pregnant. She looked to me like the kind of girl who likes to have nice things—like Janet, only not so smart."

"How do you know she's not so smart as Janet?" Lily asked.

"Because if she had been, she would never have started in with a guy like him. She would have done like Janet did, seen to it she could take care of herself. I'm telling you, girls, a good job is worth any two men in the world."

"She must be rotten if she walked out on her own kids," Lily said.

"Oh, I don't know. She can't of been more than sixteen when she got pregnant. What's a kid of sixteen know about getting buried?"

"Buried?" Marybeth asked.

"Buried—under more bills and problems and responsibilities than you can get out from under in a lifetime."

Marybeth sighed. Doris never got tired of pounding out the same message. She didn't encourage her mother to go on, but Doris did anyway. "It doesn't take much for a fifteen-, sixteen-year-old girl to get pregnant—nothing to it. One little slip and—"

54

"Mama, I told you, Peter and I are not doing anything like that."

"Don't tell me he hasn't thought about it. I've seen the way you look at him."

"How about how he looks at her?" Lily tried to defend Marybeth.

"He's not the one responsible. She's the one who's gotta keep saying 'no.' "

"Why isn't he responsible?" Marybeth asked. "It takes two to make a baby."

"Because he's just a kid, an immature kid, and you've got better sense than he has, and you know how it could be because I've told you often enough. Also, Marybeth Mason, if you have it in your foolish head that he's going to marry you if you get in trouble, forget it. His grandparents would never let him marry you even if he wanted to, which I sincerely doubt."

"Mama, why are we having this discussion now? Just because I babysat the Frazier kids today? I wish you'd stop it. I'm not the least bit like Laura Frazier, and Peter's not the little kid you think he is either."

"Yeah, you always know better. Kids always know better till it happens to them. Don't I know? Didn't the same thing happen to me?"

"You make it sound so awful now," Marybeth said resentfully. "I'll bet you loved our father when you married him."

"Sure I loved him." Her voice changed, became reminiscent, and while her eyes were on the television screen, her thoughts turned inward. "I loved your father so I thought I couldn't live without him. I couldn't stand letting him out of my sight. I couldn't say no to anything he asked of me. And what did it get me? One good year and misery ever since."

"Mama!" Marybeth burst out with the feeling she'd

55

held back for years. "Every time you talk like that, you make us wish we'd never been born."

"What do you mean? What kind of thing is that to say? *I* make you wish you'd never been born?"

"It's true," Lily chimed in. "We know if you didn't have to support us, you could buy yourself stuff like Janet does and then you'd be happy, like Janet."

"Whoever said such a thing? It's a lie! I'd never say a thing like that. Why, I wouldn't trade my girls for all the clothes and jewelry in the world!"

"You mean that, Mama?" Lily asked.

"Of course I mean it."

"It's not what you sound like you're saying," Marybeth said.

"Well, don't listen to me then. Haven't I got a right to gripe in my own house without everybody taking me so serious?" She held out her arms, and Marybeth and Lily fell into them for a long, three-way hug.

But afterward, Marybeth wasn't so sure. Which was real—what her mother had seemed to be saying all these years or what she claimed was true just now? What Doris had said now was probably what she wanted to feel all right, that her daughters were worth all the struggles she'd gone through, but—maybe, Marybeth considered, maybe both things were true. Maybe Doris wished she were free and thought her children were worth being buried for too. Why not? People were so full of contradictions. It was almost natural to want two opposing things at the same time.

Babysitting the Frazier kids was a game until Wednesday. That day's disasters started as soon as Garth Frazier left for work. Marybeth had collected piles of dirty wash to do in the washing machine. One pile of extra dirty clothes included Garth's work pants and shirts and the kids' muddied shorts and shirts. A second pile of white sheets and T-shirts awaited bleaching. A third pile held everything else. Since Eric thought the piles were great fun, he built them into mountain peaks as high as Lise's head by adding all the clean clothes from his dresser. Marybeth filled the washer and set about teaching her charges to sing "All around the mulberry bush . . ." as she cleaned up the kitchen. An hour later they all trooped down to unload the machine, but they stopped short on the basement stairs. The mountains of clothes were afloat in water, which pulsed out of a burst hose on the washing machine. Marybeth raced back upstairs with Eric still clutched under her arm to call Garth.

While Garth was on his way home, Marybeth left Eric with Lise in the kitchen and waded through the water in the basement to shut off the valve as Garth had directed her. After the water stopped pouring in, she began picking up sopping clothes, wringing them out and dropping them into a plastic laundry basket. It filled all too quickly, leaving her hands aching and a sea of floating clothing still covering the floor.

"Can't I help?" Lise called.

"What I need is an old-fashioned wringer," Marybeth said. "Do you know the kind that has two rollers that you can squeeze something between?" A little further explanation and Lise disappeared to find a wringer. Marybeth picked up another workshirt and began squeezing. Just as Lise appeared at the top of the stairs with a mop bucket with a small wringer attached to it, Marybeth heard Eric's screams. She dropped everything and raced upstairs. Eric was lying at the bottom of the bare wooden staircase to the upstairs, blood gushing from his head. Lise started screaming in sympathy with her brother.

Gingerly, Marybeth explored the cut on Eric's scalp. No question it was going to need stitches. She gently pressed the skin on either side of the wound and the blood flow diminished.

"Can you move your fingers, Eric?" she asked the now whimpering little boy. Obediently he moved his fingers to show her, then his arms, then his legs. "Where do you hurt?" she asked him.

"My head."

"Anywhere else?"

He nodded while the tears rolled placidly down his face.

"Lise, can you find me a clean towel and bring me the bottle of cold water in the refrigerator?" She knew Lise couldn't get at the ice-cube tray in the freezer, which was above the refrigerator. Shortly Lise came back complaining, "All the towels are in the wash."

Just then Garth walked in. "What happened?"

"I'm sorry," Marybeth said, afraid he was going to be furious with her. "I left him alone too long, I guess. I was trying to pick up some of the mess in the basement, and he fell down the stairs here. I wasn't thinking straight. I should have stayed with Eric and—"

"Don't, Marybeth," Garth said calmly, taking his son and feeling him all over for broken bones. "You did the best you could, better than anybody in the same situation. Hold him now, while I get some ice to stop the bleeding." He was out in the kitchen and back in a minute. Marybeth felt a tremendous relief to have him there in charge. She was glad he wasn't blaming her. She blamed herself enough. She should have had better sense than to let a two-year-old run around unsupervised.

On the way to the hospital in Garth's car, Marybeth held Eric and kept the towel-wrapped ice against his head near the wound. Garth wove the car skillfully through the traffic making good time without being reckless. Once in the emergency ward, Marybeth waited on the green plastic couch with Lise while Garth took Eric into the examining room.

"Daddy called Grandma Velum last night," Lise said.

"Who's Grandma Velum?"

"That's Mommy's mommy. I got to say hello to her."

"That's nice, Lise."

"But Grandma Velum made Daddy so mad he broke his pencil in half and then he started to cry."

"He did? Your poor daddy."

"Marybeth?"

"What, darling?"

"When's Mommy coming back?"

"I don't know."

"Well, will you stay with us then till she comes?"

"As long as I can. But I have to go to school in a week and a half."

"Will we go swimming this afternoon?"

"Eric won't be able to, but maybe you can play in the pool, and I'll sit with Eric and watch you."

"No, if Eric can't go in the pool, I won't either."

Marybeth hugged her. "You're a love, little Lise. Do you know what a love you are?"

In the car going home with Eric wearing a large bandage cap, Garth said, "Don't worry about the mess in the basement, Marybeth. I'll take care of it when I get home tonight."

He worked so hard and never complained, Marybeth thought. She looked at his haggard profile. The only remnants of youth were his winged eyebrows and blond helmet of hair. He was admirable, the way Doris was, for accepting responsibility and never giving up.

But he kept everything inside instead of letting off steam the way Doris did. Marybeth hoped he had some outlet, somebody he could talk to who sympathized with him. He seemed so alone.

"I spoke to my mother-in-law last night," he said suddenly as if he had read her mind.

"Oh? Did she say when Laura is coming home?"

"She said a lot of things. She always was against Laura marrying me. She claims it's my fault Laura left. She says she hopes she'll come back. I'm sure the old—that she knows where to find her daughter, but she won't tell me. She wouldn't even . . . You'd think one of them would give a—would care about the kids, but to hear her talk, you'd never think she was the kids' grandmother." He took a deep breath.

"I'm sorry, Marybeth. It's bad enough I've got you working when you should be out having fun without giving you an earful of my troubles besides. Look, uh—I may need you until you go back to school. Think you can stand it?"

"Oh, sure."

"Well, I may have to owe you for part of your pay. Not for too long though. I'm looking for a second job. Oh, and I wrote to an aunt of mine. She's a single woman. Lives as companion to an old lady, and I know she wants out of that. She might agree to take over the kids until Laura comes back—if she ever comes back."

"Don't worry, Garth. I hope Laura comes back soon, but in the meantime you can count on me. And you don't have to pay me a thing. I'm having a ball taking care of the kids."

"Had a ball this morning too?" he asked, grinning.

"Well, not this morning. No." She had to laugh at herself.

By the time he got home for his dinner that night,

she had run the wet laundry through the clothes wringer and laid it out neatly to be washed when the machine was fixed—all except for the few essential pieces she had washed by hand and hung on the back line to dry in the late afternoon sun.

Her reward for the day's labors came when Lily came limping across the street. Her limp was always exaggerated whenever she rushed. She had an impish grin on her face and a letter in her hand. "Guess who this is from!"

"Peter!" Marybeth screamed and grabbed the letter and slit it open with the one unbroken nail she had left.

"He never wrote you a real letter before. He must really miss you," Lily said. Peter's large, childish scrawl filled the page with just a few lines. Marybeth began reading aloud.

Dear Marybeth,

I told you I was going to write a real letter this time and here it is. Well there isn't much to write about because it's boring here with nothing to do but fish and swim. If you were here it wouldn't be boring—you know why. I tried to take the sailboat out two days in a row but there wasn't any wind. The biggest thing was catching a snapping turtle yesterday. I call him Sam and he eats raw meat from my fingers and he'd eat my fingers too if I let him. I wish I had my motorcycle here. I've been bugging Grandpa to get me a shotgun instead. You be good now and think of me and don't go out with any other guys while I'm gone and remember to write every day. I read all your letters twice and I love you and miss you a lot.

Love, Peter

Marybeth smiled. The weariness of the day fell away from her like a cast-off skin. "He misses me," she said.

Lily wrinkled her nose. "What's he want a shotgun for?"

"Oh, you know Peter. He always has to have a new toy."

"Is he going to kill things with it?"

"I don't know, Lily. I'll tell him you're worried when I write."

"Don't do *that*. He'll know I read his letter."

Marybeth giggled. "You think he wouldn't know that anyway?"

"Mama wants you to hurry up and help her," Lily said. "Janet's coming over for dinner tonight, you know."

Marybeth groaned. "You'd think once in a while she could invite Mama for dinner instead of it always being the other way around."

"Mama doesn't care. She thinks anything Janet does is fine."

"I know."

"And besides, if Janet invited Mama for dinner, she'd have to invite us too. Can you imagine Janet making dinner for all of us?"

"I can't imagine Janet doing anything for anybody but herself," Marybeth said.

Doris was flustered. "Where were you, Marybeth? Janet's due any minute and I don't have anything started. I just laid down for a catnap after work and I slept right through till five-thirty."

"I'll do the salad. Lily can set the table," Marybeth said. "And Janet can wait if she comes. Stop rushing around, Mama. She's family not company."

To Doris's relief, Janet was late, which made the

dinner on time. They all sat down at the kitchen table and ate their canned fruit salad immediately.

"Something I want you to look at," Janet said, passing a photograph from her purse across the table to Doris. "What do you think of that place?"

"It's a nice-looking cottage, honey, and with a lake right behind it, huh?"

"It's smack on the lake, and they say there's a clean sand beach close by, and the town is within walking distance. What do you think of it?"

"I thought you said you weren't going to go away this summer. You said you were going to the Caribbean in November instead."

"I am, but this is something besides that. What do you think, girls? Doesn't your mama need a vacation?"

"She certainly does," Marybeth said.

"Sure she does," Lily said. "I do too."

"Me?" Doris said. "I can't afford to go around the corner. Where am I going to get the cash to go anyplace?"

"You could if it was cheap enough, couldn't you? Like for four days over Labor Day weekend. How does that sound?"

"Oh, I could never get off over Labor Day. That's a busy time at the restaurant. They'd never give me time off then."

"Doris! When did you take a vacation last?"

"Christmas. I stayed home Christmas week."

"Well, but when did you go anywheres during the summer?"

"I don't know. That time we went to New York City for a day."

"Big deal!" Janet said. "Your boss will give you time off if you ask him. And you know how much this place costs a week?"

"I haven't the faintest idea."

"It goes for two-hundred-and-fifty dollars."

"That's ridiculous—for us."

"*And*—give me a chance to finish—*and* the guy who rented it can only use it for three days. So he says if I want it for a hundred for the four-day weekend, I can have it. So right away I thought of you. Look, we split it fifty-fifty. You can afford fifty dollars, Doris."

Doris considered. "Yeah, I guess. Where is the place?"

"Just a two-hour drive. We could go in your four door and I'll pay the gas."

"Would you girls like it?"

"Yes!" Lily shouted.

"I doubt I'll be able to go," Marybeth said.

"Why not?"

"Well, I told Garth Frazier I'd stay with his kids until school started. Unless he can get his aunt to come in time, or if his wife should come back, but I couldn't just go and leave the kids without anyone to take care of them."

"We're not going unless we all go," Doris said.

"Why, Mama? I don't mind staying back to babysit. I'd feel terrible to have you miss a vacation. You really deserve one."

"You know I wouldn't leave you home alone with that man across the street."

"What man?"

"What man? Garth Frazier. Who else?"

"Oh, Mama, don't be silly. He's the nicest person."

"Don't be silly? You don't know what you're talking about. He's a man and you're a girl."

"An old married man, Mama."

"He's not old. What would you say he is, Janet, twenty-five, twenty-six?"

"Let's see. His brother that got killed was in my

class in high school. I'd say Garth is maybe twenty-four, twenty-five."

"There you go, Miss. Less than ten years—no difference to speak of between a man and a girl, and I'm not leaving you here alone with him."

"All right. What I'll do is ask him to see if he can get his aunt here fast. But if he can't, I can't go."

"Well, we'll see about that. It's not your responsibility to care for those children," Janet said butting in.

"I'll stay home with you, Marybeth," Lily said sadly.

"No, Lily. It would be fun for you to go away. You've never had a chance to go anywhere much."

"Nobody's going unless we all go," Doris said again.

"I'm so disappointed," Janet said. "Here I thought you'd all be so happy. A whole vacation for just fifty dollars and gas and whatever the food comes to."

"The food?" Lily asked.

"Yes. The cottage has a kitchen so we can eat in and save money that way. Actually, you can't even count the food cost because you'd be paying it whether you're home or away."

"You mean Mama has to cook?" Lily said. "That's no vacation for her."

"I don't mind. We'll all pitch in," Doris said.

"Who pays for the groceries?" Lily asked.

Marybeth blushed at her sister's nerviness and Doris reproached her. "Lily! What's the matter with you? There're three of us and only a little size ten of Janet. What she eats isn't worth mentioning."

Marybeth saw Lily's eyes go to Janet's plate, where their mother had dished out the same portions the rest of them got, but for once Lily held her tongue.

"Maybe Janet would take us all out for pizza one night and that could be her share of the food costs,"

Marybeth suggested and was tickled when her aunt reluctantly admitted that that sounded fair enough.

Marybeth was so tired that night that she couldn't sleep. She lay there stewing about how she was going to manage to take care of the Frazier kids as she had promised and go to the lake with her family as Doris insisted. She wouldn't mind a vacation at the lake, even if Peter wasn't going to be there with her, but what she was really looking forward to most was the first day of school when she had Peter back.

As she did every night just before she fell asleep, she conjured Peter up until he was lying there beside her. Then she whispered out loud the words dammed up inside her, "Peter, my own, my darling. I love you so." Soon inside the cocoon of her thoughts, his hands began to move over her body and her nerve endings began to thrill to his touch. Inside the safe bounds of her own thoughts, it was impossible to stop the love-making that seemed to have a flow as natural as the river and an even more powerful current. Soon, she thought, soon they would be together again.

Chapter 5

The shorter the time to Peter's return, the more Marybeth ached to see him. He filled her mind so that the shape of everything was Peter. The hint of his stride in the mailman's footsteps made her heart skip. The chestnut glint in the hair of a man pruning the elm near the highway sent her racing to see if he could be Peter home early after all. She was too wrought up over his return to be able to feel much about anything else. The game of playing house with Garth's children had settled into an everyday routine with an equal mix of pleasures and difficulties. Eric had days when he woke up crabby, refused to get dressed, said "no" to everything she offered him to eat, and then would do something like wail for an hour when she wouldn't let him take his dirt truck into the newly scrubbed plastic swimming pool. Even Lise could be difficult. She didn't like it when Eric touched her bride doll. "He messes her up," she said and would pinch him hard if she caught him pulling at the ribbon around the doll's waist. Then Eric screamed and Marybeth had to make peace by quickly distracting them with another activity.

By the time Garth's Aunt Florence arrived, Marybeth was ready to pass the responsibility for the children to her, except that the huge woman looked so forbidding. She had small, wary eyes like weapons, bulbous arms and legs and a stomach that bulged out to her knees as she sat on the couch. While Marybeth described the routines, likes and dislikes of the children, Aunt Florence listened impassively and made no comment.

Then Marybeth offered, "Would you like me to stay today and help you get started?"

"I can handle them," the woman said and never budged while Marybeth kissed Lise and Eric goodbye, reminding them that she would be just across the street if they wanted her. Lise clung to Marybeth's waist, obviously afraid of Florence. Eric copied his sister even to the tears.

"You be good for your Aunt Florence now," Marybeth said and pried their hands loose and left them. Probably, she thought, the woman was just shy and would warm up to the children once she was alone with them. That had to be why Florence hadn't wanted Marybeth to hang around and help her get started. She was just shy. So Marybeth quieted her own uneasiness.

At home the atmosphere was happily hectic. Doris and Lily were preparing for the four-day vacation as if it were a European tour. Clothes had to be dragged out, considered, repaired or washed, then packed. Big decisions had to be discussed: Should they drag along the portable barbecue and the charcoal briquets? What was Lily going to do without a bathing suit? Maybe they should get new batteries and take the flashlight along.

"Why are you so quiet, Marybeth? Aren't you glad you're going on vacation?" Lily asked.

"Sure I am," Marybeth said, but the truth was she would gladly have given up her part of it to bring Peter home sooner.

They settled in at their vacation cottage under a soughing canopy of spicy scented pines, whose needles padded the surrounding earth and provided shade from the sun that glittered off the lake. To Marybeth's delight, vacation turned Doris into a fun-loving child again. She chased Lily all around the porch one evening yelling that a bear was after her while Lily screeched in mock terror. It was Doris who turned out to be the most graceful the night Janet tried to teach them all to do a hula dance she had learned in Hawaii. They laughed so much that night that Lily got the hiccups. Even Janet was fun to be with. Marybeth was so grateful, she squeezed her aunt's hand and thanked her warmly for thinking up the vacation idea. Doris announced on the way home, "That was the best vacation I ever had."

All day Wednesday, Marybeth fluttered about watching the Josselyns' house, expecting their car to pull in any minute. "Where can they be?" she asked Lily a dozen times. School started Thursday. The summer was over. She couldn't endure waiting for him another minute.

Finally, after dinner the screen door flew open, and there stood Peter. Without even looking at him, Marybeth threw herself into his arms. They tried to bridge the two weeks they had been apart with their kiss. Doris was working, but Lily was very much present. All evening she kept appearing in the living room with offers of food or soda or juice until Peter said,

"Lily, isn't it past your bedtime? There's school tomorrow. Go to bed, huh?"

"I don't think I should leave you alone here," Lily said looking at them anxiously as they sat there on the couch tangled in each other's arms.

"Lily, please," Marybeth begged. "We need to be alone. Just, please, leave us be for tonight."

Lily hesitated. "If I go to my room, are you going to be good, Marybeth?"

Marybeth nodded. "I'll be good, but don't you come down to check on us anymore. Okay?"

Lily dragged herself up the stairs reluctantly. Marybeth felt like a bottle of soda, so fluid and fizzy with excitement. Lily's bedroom door clicked shut. Peter and Marybeth began discarding clothes immediately. Neither said a word. Neither could have stopped. The impulse was irresistible. In a minute the delicious feel of naked flesh on flesh blotted out all thought. Then the telephone shrilled. Marybeth jerked upright. Peter cursed.

"Don't answer it," he said.

"Have to," she said, and slipped into the sundress she had been wearing and dashed into the kitchen. It was Doris to say she was going to be late.

"Don't wait up, honey. You have school tomorrow. Did Peter get home yet?"

"Yes."

"Okay. Then you behave yourself, you hear?"

"Yes," Marybeth repeated.

"We could go up to your room," Peter whispered when she came back.

She looked down at the beautiful, naked length of him stretched out on the sofa and wanted so badly to kiss his body over inch by precious inch that she nearly lost the resolve the phone call had given her.

"You have to get up and go home," she said. "*Now,* Peter. I'll see you at the bus stop tomorrow."

"Marybeth, don't act this way. What's the matter with you? You know I can't stand much more of this. I need you so much."

"No more than I need you," she said and stood at arm's length handing him his clothes. Peter was angry at her when he left.

"Some welcome home!" he complained.

It made her feel rotten. Not even the satisfaction of knowing she hadn't let her mother down helped, and she wondered how long God was going to go on protecting her from herself. Two years of miraculous intervention until they graduated from high school seemed a lot to expect.

Chapter 6

Marybeth always made an effort to be friendly toward newcomers in her classes, especially if they looked at all shy, but she hadn't even spoken to Hillary. No need to put her at ease. Hillary breezed into their lives with a big smile, acting as if everyone around already was her friend. She was attractive, well dressed, and confident—not a girl who needed support from Marybeth. That was why Marybeth was surprised when one week into the term while they were standing in the cafeteria line, Peter said, "Hey, guess what? We're going to a pool party Saturday."

"We are? Where?"

"At Hillary's house."

"I don't even know her, Peter."

"That's okay. She invited us both."

"But how come she invited us?"

"Oh, she sits next to me in French. We've talked. Anyway, a whole bunch of kids are going. It should be great. We've never been to a pool party before."

"I don't even know anyone who has a pool except a kiddie pool."

"This isn't a kiddie pool. She says it's Olympic size, and they're going to have hamburgers and stuff for dinner and entertainment and everything. Isn't that great?"

71

Marybeth raised her eyebrows when he named the street where Hillary lived. No wonder the girl seemed to have everything. She lived on Devon Road, where all the doctors and lawyers and big store owners lived. Marybeth was curious to see the inside of a house on Devon Road. It had to look like a movie set. "I'll ask Mama if I can go," she said.

"Oh, she'll let you go," Peter said confidently.

"Do we have to bring anything?"

"Hillary said just a swimsuit and towel."

"I still don't know how to swim, Peter."

"Didn't you learn on your vacation?"

"In four days?"

"Well, you can lie around looking pretty and watch me showing off. How's that?"

"Sounds good." She smiled affectionately at his happy face. She hoped he would like the way she looked in the bikini her mother had made for her last summer. It had faded to a blotchy, pinkish red, and she couldn't trust it not to fall off in the water so it was just as well she couldn't swim since she wouldn't dare go in a pool in it. "Are you going to wear your hat?" she asked him.

"My hat?"

"Your birthday present. Did you forget already?"

"No, but—I left it in New Hampshire, Marybeth. Are you mad at me?"

"No." She had wondered why he hadn't been wearing it. "You will get it back though, won't you?"

"Oh, sure," he said.

Doris made a face when Marybeth told her where the party was. "Devon Road!" she said. "What've you got in common with anyone there?"

"Oh, Mama! People from Devon Road can be nice too. Anyway, it's a big party, and she's invited lots of people."

The afternoon of the party, Doris handed over her best towel, a thick blue one she saved for Janet's use. "You better take this, Marybeth. I don't want anyone making fun of you. All our other towels are worn through."

"Mama, nobody's going to make fun of me. People don't care if we have less money than they do."

"So you say."

"Nobody could make fun of Marybeth," Lily said staunchly. "She looks just like a movie star."

"That bikini's so baggy. If I had the time, I'd sew you another one. I don't know why you didn't buy a new one on sale like I told you to."

"Mama, please stop worrying. Everything's going to be all right."

"I think she looks sexy," Lily said.

"Now what kind of thing is that to say to your sister?" Doris said. "Some ideas you have in your head, Lily Mason!"

Lily blushed and then pouted. Marybeth laughed. She changed into jeans and a T-shirt and waited for Peter to pick her up. His grandfather was driving them.

Hillary's house was as impressive as Marybeth had imagined. It had a gray stone front with a big screened-in porch on one side and a large two-door garage on the other, all set way back from the road behind a lawn full of cultivated trees and shrubs. Sounds of laughter from the backyard drew them from the driveway around the garage on a pebbled walk to the back. There the land fell away in terraces, starting with a stone patio at the top and going on down to the fenced-in pool way at the back behind a grove of trees.

"It's gorgeous!" Marybeth exclaimed.

"Nice," Peter said, hurrying ahead of her toward the pool. The pool was surrounded by a deck with plastic lawn chairs and small live bushes set in redwood tubs. Hillary appeared like a genie from the crowd of kids. Marybeth was flattered at being singled out for a greeting.

"Hi, you two. Glad you could come. If you're thirsty, there's an ice chest of soda and beer over there. The program's simple—swimming, then eating and dancing. Later tonight a friend of my mother's who's a really great guitarist is going to play for us."

Marybeth smiled at Hillary. In her white string bikini with her wet hair plastered back to show the fine, high cheekbones which were her best feature, Hillary looked wonderful. "You have a beautiful house, Hillary," Marybeth said. "I never knew a swimming pool could be so pretty."

"Glad you like it." Her glance slid past Marybeth to Peter. "You can change in the shed over there, Pete. Girls use the laundry room, Marybeth. Just go through the sliding glass doors at the back of the house and turn right." Hillary leaned sideways and wrung out her hair saying, "You look like a swimmer, Peter. Are you?"

"I like to dive," Peter said.

"Really? I knew we had a lot in common. I'm a diver too. Meet you on the board then. We're having a competition—just for fun."

All of a sudden Marybeth understood why she had been invited. Hillary liked Peter! Marybeth had only been included in the invitation because she and Peter were a couple. She looked after Peter, who was on his way to the shed to change. She turned away from the pool of noisy, splashing kids and trudged across the lawn toward the house, fighting a sense of uneasiness. As she walked, she gave herself a talking-to. What did it matter if Hillary hadn't invited her for her own sake? After all, Hillary didn't even know her. If Marybeth wanted to change that, it was up to her to make friends with Hillary. As to Peter, naturally other girls were going to flirt with him. He was so cute. It would be silly to panic every time some girl showed she liked him. They had been faithful to each other for five years, longer than some marriages lasted, for heaven's sake. She had nothing to worry about.

The laundry room was strewn with girls' clothing. Marybeth shucked her pants and T-shirt, deciding, as she looked over the clothes around her, that she'd made a mistake not to dress up more. She could have looked pretty much like the others if only she'd known what they would be wearing. She caught sight of herself in the mirror over the sink in the small bathroom that stood open into the laundry room and was dismayed to see how very white her skin looked. She sucked in her stomach and nearly lost the bottom of her bikini. It did look homemade and saggy. She should have let her mother spend the money for a new one. She squeezed at her thighs, which already seemed to be getting flabby like her mother's. If only she tanned! But all her time in the sun this summer had left only a faint beige color on her arms and the pale design of strap marks on her shoulders. How could Lily think she was pretty? It was just love that made her see Marybeth that way. What she looked like was a marshmallow with wispy, dirty blond hair and a nondescript face so ordinary that teachers always learned her name last in any class. She thought of Hillary's distinctive looks. Not that she was so pretty, but she was different enough so you remembered her. And where Marybeth was soft and white, Hillary was taut and tanned. A sound made Marybeth turn from her self-scrutiny. A girl stood watching her. She knew this girl from school somewhere.

"Hi," Marybeth said.

"Hi. Would you mind if I used the bathroom?"

"Oh, sorry." She stepped out of the way, embarrassed. Now she remembered the girl, who wore one long braid down her back and a skin-tight racing suit over a compact body. She had been in Marybeth's math class in freshman year, a girl who never talked and rarely smiled, but she was smart.

"How's the water?" Marybeth asked as the girl slipped past her into the bathroom.

"Okay. Too many kids fooling around in it though. You can't really swim. You're with a boy, aren't you?"

"Yes."

"Lucky. I'm here by myself. My mother made me come, but I knew it was no good." She shrugged. "I'm lousy at these things."

"Pool parties?"

"Social things—any kind of social thing."

"When you don't know anyone, it's hard. I don't know anyone here either."

"But you have a boy, so it doesn't matter."

"I guess so. Look, why don't you come and sit with me and Peter? You can be with us. He's friendly."

"Thanks," the girl said. "But I think I'll just call my mother and tell her I have a stomachache."

Marybeth went back to the pool area alone feeling self-conscious. She wished the girl had come with her, especially when she saw that Peter was already poised on the diving board with an admiring bevy of kids at the edge of the pool to watch him. He flipped up into the air and revolved like a corkscrew burrowing down into the water. When his head popped out everybody clapped, including Marybeth.

"And next we have our hostess, Miss Hillary Shultes," a male voice announced through an improvised megaphone.

Hillary stood sleek as a porpoise balancing at the end of the board concentrating too hard to notice everyone's eyes on her. All at once she launched into a backward somersault. Marybeth gasped with admiration.

"And now for your divertissement, ladies and gentlemen, and all you others out there," the megaphone voice went on. "Here is our very own, Felix the clown."

A skinny boy crept shivering to the edge of the board, made scared eyes at the audience and peered over, bending so that it looked as if he must surely fall. Then he backed up pretending fearful indecision. The kids whistled at him and urged him to jump. Finally the crowd started counting, "One, two, three . . ." After the clown jumped, Marybeth smiled and looked around for someone with whom to start a conversation. Peter had disappeared entirely. She recognized faces from grade school, but none of them had ever been her particular friends. She said, "Hi, Lori," to one smiling, curly-haired girl.

The girl looked at her in surprise and tried to remember her name. "Hi, there," she said.

"I'm Marybeth," Marybeth helped her out. "We were in third grade together."

"Oh, right. Hi. Been in the water yet?"

"Not yet."

"It's nice. You ought to go in." She continued on her way to a group of kids who were sitting on the grass outside the pool's fence.

Marybeth looked around for someone else to talk to. Everyone seemed to be occupied either swimming, talking, or eating. A golden retriever stood nose to the fence wagging a plumy tail, his eyes fixed on Marybeth. "Hi, there," she said to him and walked around the fence to pet him. His was the only friendly face in sight. He rolled over on his back in ecstasy at her attentions. "You're sure a nice fella," she crooned as she scratched his belly. "Such a good dog, yes, you are. I once had a dog like you." The pain flashed anew as she remembered Tickles chasing the ball she had thrown for Lily, chasing it out onto the highway and his slim, amber body flying through the air when the car hit him and Lily's hysteria which wasn't controlled until the doctor prescribed a sedative for her. "No more pets," Doris had said after Tickles, and then with finality after the stray collie they took in had been killed on that same highway. The golden retriever yawned, and stood up, looking up at her to see what she wanted to do next. But he wasn't the companion she had come to this party for. Where was Peter? She felt abandoned, and to keep the feeling from overwhelming her, she set off to find him.

Music drew her toward the house. Maybe he had gone inside. She considered searching in there for him, but felt odd about walking around inside in her bikini. The pool area now looked almost deserted. Only two boys were left swimming, making great splashes in the water, and one couple engrossed in conversation with each other. Where had the party gone? Marybeth wandered toward the grove of trees. Tables had been set up near a brick barbecue pit there, and sure enough, that was where everyone had migrated. She ran, eager to find Peter and belong again.

He was standing beside Hillary turning hamburgers on a grill. Marybeth almost didn't recognize him in the chef's high, white hat and large apron he was wearing. Hillary had on a costume too. It looked like a printed tablecloth tied around her chest and under one armpit. Somehow Hillary looked graceful and sexy in it. The open side exposed the naked length of her crossed by the string of the bikini bottom. Marybeth threw her arms around Peter and clung, her spirits rising now that she had found him. "Why didn't you tell me where you were going, Peter? I didn't know where you were," she said.

He shook her off by shrugging his shoulders. Perplexed, she stepped back and looked at him. His grin was embarrassed, but it wasn't directed at her, but at the lineup of kids waiting for their hamburgers. What was wrong with him? He'd never been embarrassed when they hugged each other in school. Marybeth's eyes cruised the faces around the barbecue—sly grins, barely hidden smiles as if something were funny all at once about her showing affection toward Peter. She didn't understand it. What she did understand was that for the first time in five years Peter was not with her, but with them, with those strangers waiting in line with paper plates in their hands, with Hillary, who stood beside him calmly flipping burgers onto plates.

"Marybeth," he said in a joking voice, "what's the matter with you? Can't you find someone to talk to?"

"I have been talking to people," she said defensively.

"Well, that's why I couldn't find you then. You want to help with these hamburgers now you're here?"

"Sure."

"I'll find you an apron," Hillary offered. She ran off looking like a Polynesian girl on some exotic island. A sarong, Marybeth thought. That must be what Hillary was wearing. Feeling too exposed in her bikini, too naked and fleshy, too soft and white, she sucked in her stomach. Automatically she began picking up patties of meat to replace the cooked ones that had been served from the grill.

"Hey!" Peter said. "Don't touch the meat without washing your hands first."

"My hands aren't dirty." But then she remembered

playing with the dog. "All right. I'll go wash and be right back." She ran off to the bathroom in the laundry room, but someone was in there. While she waited, she put on her jeans and shirt, not so glamorous as a sarong, but it covered her at least.

A misery had settled in her chest. Peter was acting odd, as if other people now mattered more to him than she did, as if she were in the way. She shook her head at herself. Didn't she scold Lily for being supersensitive?

The bathroom door opened finally. The girl who came out looked as if she had been crying. She glanced at Marybeth, dropped her eyes and slunk away. Poor thing, Marybeth thought as she washed her hands, used the toilet, washed her hands again and looked herself in the eyes in the mirror. "Cheer up," she told herself, "and act like you're having a good time." That would bring Peter around a lot better than moping. She made herself smile and carried the smile back to the barbecue area with her.

Few people were left waiting for hamburgers to cook. Hillary stood facing Peter, swaying provocatively in time to the music that wafted into the yard from somewhere in the house.

"You sure took your time, Marybeth," Peter said. "We're just about done."

"I brought you an apron," Hillary said. "But there's really no need now. Thanks anyway."

"Sorry," Marybeth said, still smiling. "There was a girl in the bathroom. I—" She stopped. Why make excuses when she hadn't done anything wrong? Neither one of them noticed her unfinished sentence.

"Time for the cooks to eat," Peter said. "How about it, Hillary?"

"Actually I'm a vegetarian," Hillary said.

"You are?"

80

"Um hum. I'll just have some of the salads. Want me to fix you a plate, Peter?"

"Marybeth'll take care of it." He scooped two hamburgers onto two buns.

"Just mustard on mine," Marybeth said, and moved toward the table laden with bowls of potato and macaroni and tossed salads. There she knew what to do. It was much like a church supper. She picked up two paper plates, humming to keep her spirits up, and loaded one with everything for Peter. On the second plate she took some macaroni for herself. But when she turned around, they were gone again. The grill was deserted. Picnicking kids sat all around the lawn, but she didn't see Peter and Hillary. She started back toward the pool trying to convince herself it was really sort of funny the way the party kept getting away from her, but she wasn't amused.

She spotted them finally in the pool area, sitting at an umbrella table together. Peter was laughing as an animated Hillary told him some story with much waving of her hands. It was strange how Hillary appeared more attractive every time Marybeth looked at her. Marybeth set her plates down on their table and dragged a wet deck chair over for herself. She sat down on the edge of it.

"Thanks," Peter said, moving the plate of salads in front of him and beginning to eat.

"You're welcome. Where's my hamburger?"

"Oh, I'm sorry. I ate it. It was getting cold anyways. There's more by the grill. Want me to get you one?"

"That's okay. I'm not very hungry." She dug her fork into her macaroni, which appeared to be all she was going to get to eat, and realized that it was true; she wasn't hungry anymore. She forced the smile she had lost back onto her lips and asked, "What were you laughing about as I came up?"

81

"Laughing?" Peter echoed.

"Hillary was telling you something that made you laugh."

"Oh, that was nothing," Hillary said.

"This stuff tastes great, Hillary," Peter said. "Did you cook any of it?"

"Not a speck. Mom and I just cleaned out the delicatessen."

"How come you became a vegetarian?" Marybeth asked, edging her way into the conversation.

"It started with my older brother whom I adore," Hillary said. "He was a vegey. And then I got to reading about how wasteful we are to eat meat. It uses up so much grain and grass and energy and stuff to produce every pound of meat we buy at the butcher, and that grain could feed hordes of starving people in the world. I began feeling sort of guilty, you know? Then what clinched it was I really liked vegetarian dishes when I tried them. I feel better eating them, so much lighter and cleaner. Of course, I don't think vegetarianism is for everyone. A guy like Peter could no more be a vegey than a lion could. He's too red-blooded—a real he-man."

"Peter?" Marybeth blurted out in surprise. She checked to see if her boyish beloved had changed into a he-man while she wasn't looking. He looked the same, but his grin told her Hillary's image had flattered him.

The music, Marybeth could now see, was coming from speakers around the pool. She swayed her shoulders in time to the catchy rhythm and looked at Peter hoping he would feel like dancing.

"Marybeth, would you mind if I borrowed Peter for a little while?" Hillary asked. "I want to start the kids dancing, and you know how hard that kind of thing is to start unless somebody's doing it."

"Peter and I can start the dancing for you," Marybeth offered. "You're brave enough to be first, aren't you, Peter?"

"Not me," Peter said. "I'm not going to be first."

"All right, you guys. You wait here then," Hillary said. She took off leaving them to sit in the first uncomfortable silence that had ever fallen between them. In five minutes Hillary returned, driving most of the guests before her in genial roundup. She began dancing by herself. "Come on, everybody. Let's dance!" The clown joined her. He could really move!

"Peter, aren't you going to dance with me?" Marybeth asked.

"Not now."

He wouldn't look at her. Instead they kept their eyes on the dancers, who had multiplied into a sizable group. Marybeth kept flexing her upper body to the music. She loved dancing, and Peter was very good at it. What was the matter with him? He sat stubbornly. She touched his hand.

"Is something wrong?" she asked.

"Stop that, Marybeth," he said. "I've gotta go to the john."

While he was gone, she sat watching. Stop what? Stop caring about him all of a sudden? If someone asked her to dance, she would say yes, she decided rebelliously. But nobody asked her. She felt invisible. Out of the corner of her eye she saw Hillary take Peter's arm as he stepped through the gate to the pool area, and then they were dancing. Marybeth felt as if someone had thrown a bucket of ice cubes over her.

On the way home that night in the back of his grandfather's car, he broke the silence between them asking, "You want to tell me what you're mad about?"

"Who said I'm mad?"

"You're not talking to me."

83

"I don't notice you saying much to me."

"Look, I'm sorry I started dancing with Hillary, but she asked me, and she invited us to the party, after all. I didn't want to say no to her."

"I see."

"What do you mean, 'you see'?"

"She's a very attractive girl."

"I wish you weren't so jealous, Marybeth."

"I never had to be before, did I, Peter?"

"You don't have to be now."

But she didn't believe him, and after he kissed her goodnight at her door, she realized she had forgotten her mother's good blue towel. She could call Hillary first thing in the morning, but in her heart she knew the towel would never be found. Neither would a lot of things lost at that party.

Chapter 7

They were walking home from church on a varnished blue September morning, past empty fields studded with purple and yellow and white flowers.

"What happened at the pool party?" Lily asked.

"Nothing," Marybeth said. "What should have happened? It was just a party."

"No, it wasn't."

"Oh, Lily!"

"If nothing happened, why do you look so sad?"

"Well, it wasn't the greatest time I ever had. You can't really enjoy a pool party when you can't swim."

"Did you have a fight with Peter?"

"No."

"All right, if you don't want to tell me, don't then. . . . You used to tell me everything."

Marybeth sighed. "I can't tell you everything anymore. I'm too old, and the truth is, I can't explain what was wrong. Just I felt funny."

"How funny?"

"Please, Lily. I can't talk about it." She ignored Lily's pout and tried not to care when Lily wouldn't speak to her at lunch.

All afternoon Marybeth got jounced about on the back of Peter's motorcycle as he rode monotonously round and round a maze of trails, bumpy trails through dry fields tangled in the peacock blooms of summer's end. She couldn't have been closer to him physically, but there was a distance between them. She knew he would deny it. He preferred feelings in black and white. If she pointed to a shading in their relationship, he would claim not to see it and accuse her of being oversensitive. One thing she was going to tell him though and that was that she hated riding his motorcycle.

When he made a pit stop at the garage behind his grandparents' house to tinker with the bike's mechanisms, she began hinting. "Whew," she said, "is my bottom ever sore!"

"From what?" He was crouched beside the wheel working a nut loose with a wrench.

"From riding the bike, I guess."

"Marybeth! We were only out a little while. Don't you like riding with me?"

"Oh, Peter. I like doing anything with you, even riding your cycle." She smiled at him fondly, but he frowned back.

"You mean you don't like it."

"Well, it's not my favorite thing to do."

"You don't have to ride with me, you know." He pushed at the nut, which refused to turn. She watched him struggle and said carefully,

"I like being with you no matter what you do and where you go."

There was a long silence during which the metal agonized out loud and finally gave way to the wrench. "I'll tell you," he said without looking at her. "I think it's time we did some things separately anyway. We have to develop our potential more. It's not good to be always hanging on to each other. It keeps us from really developing our potential, you know what I mean?"

She heard the echo of someone else's words in that speech. Whose words? She didn't know how to answer him. "I didn't know I was holding you back from anything, Peter."

"You're not. Now don't get upset." He stood up. His eyes turned soft as he looked at her. "I don't want you to think I'm saying something I'm not. I still love you."

"You do?"

"Sure, I do."

"As long as you love me, everything's all right." She put her arms around him and nuzzled his cheek.

"But we do need to get more space, you know? We need more space to develop—"

"Our potential," she finished for him trying to smile about it.

The weeks passed and their relationship seemed to change with the season. They no longer spent their lunch times in school alone with each other. Hillary and the members of Hillary's newly formed clique joined them as a matter of course. Personal exchanges about the day's anxieties and goofups were no longer fit topics of conversation with the group around them. Instead, Peter told anecdotes about the surprise quiz in social studies on which someone had been caught cheating or the dead fish in the girls' locker room. His anecdotes sounded like imitations of Hillary, who seemed to be able to turn anything into an amusing story, using her mobile eyebrows and expressive hands to draw exclamation marks everywhere. Marybeth said very little in the group. Neither her ready sympathy nor her easygoing pleasantries fitted their conversation. They mocked everything—the nasal voice of the Phys. Ed. teacher, the naive remarks of a girl who had gotten pregnant, the way a boy wore his jeans belted too high. Everybody seemed ridiculous to them, or stupid. And Peter, who had once accepted people as they were, now went along with the group.

One morning when Home Ec class let out, Peter was not waiting for her. Marybeth went down to the cafeteria alone and got in line behind a girl she'd known casually for years.

"Marybeth, did you and Peter break up or something?" the girl asked.

"No. Why should you think that?"

"Oh. I just thought because I see him cutting English sometimes and going out in the woods—you know, where the kids go to smoke and drink."

"I didn't know he cut class."

"Yeah, well, it's probably that Hillary. She's the one he hangs out there with."

Marybeth picked up her tray and walked like a sleepwalker to the narrow wing of the cafeteria where Hillary had established territorial rights. There her partying crowd collected. They adhered to one another not because of likenesses or mutual interests or shared labels, but because each week one of them gave a party. Their weekend party, past or future, was another staple of conversation at lunch. It seemed to Marybeth that the parties had become pretty routine, a few hours of beer-drinking, some pot-smoking, aimless teasing and listening to music. She got through them by walking around with an untasted can of beer as a prop, seeking out the odd person who was in the mood to talk honestly about their family or, failing anything personal, last night's television shows. She had irritated Peter at last week's party by telling him he was drinking too much.

"Marybeth, you're a bore," he had said. The jolt of anger she felt in response almost made her call her mother and ask to be picked up on Doris's way home from the diner. She didn't call though. Once her anger cooled, she began to fear that walking out on him would only make Peter glad. She felt him pulling away from her, and her desperate instinct was to hang on. They were a couple. He had once appreciated the wonder of that the way she did. What was she to do now? Just let him go as if he didn't matter to her anymore? She knew other boys existed who would be interested in her, and they might even be better people than Peter, but he was the shape of love to her. No one else could ever be quite as he was. She would not let go as if what they had was insignificant.

Peter was sitting next to Hillary in the middle of the long table crowded with kids. He looked like just another laughing member of the group while Marybeth felt as if she stood out like a gold front tooth among them. "Any room for me?" she asked.

"Sure, Marybeth. Put your tray down. You can shove in here," Peter said.

"We just decided on a super project, Marybeth," Hillary said. "Some of us are going to make a movie about how kids our age see the world. Isn't that a great idea?"

"Sounds like fun," Marybeth said. "When are you going to start?"

"Oh, we'll meet Saturday afternoons at my house. Are you interested?"

"Yes, but Saturday afternoons I have a baby-sitting job."

"You could change it around."

"I don't think so. See, this woman has a retarded son. She can't leave him with just anybody. He listens to me."

"Oh, well, good for you. I'm impressed."

"With what?" Marybeth took a bite of her sandwich.

"That you're not so possessive of Peter as I thought you were," Hillary said. "I mean, I was getting the impression you'd do anything rather than let him out of your sight. That's good that you won't change your sitting plans. It really is. It's so unhealthy when kids try to possess each other. It keeps them from realizing their potential."

The words clicked in Marybeth's brain. Peter had talked about potential weeks ago. She had thought then that he was copying someone else's words. Now she knew whose. "I don't think Peter and I have held each other back from anything," Marybeth said. "I think mostly we've helped each other."

"My father says forming close bonds with a member of the opposite sex at a very early age is a sign of dependency."

"Your father?"

"He's a psychiatrist."

"Oh."

"Does that scare you? It makes a lot of people nervous when they know my father's a psychiatrist."

"Why should your father's job matter to me? I mean, I don't see any connection."

"Because I know so much about what makes people tick from listening to him."

"Do you think so?" Marybeth said. "What time are you meeting Saturdays?" she asked suddenly. "Maybe I can get over for part of it anyway." Hillary didn't know everything about people whatever her father had taught her. When it came to feelings, Marybeth trusted her own understanding over the clever theories of professionals. It had occurred to her that the house where she babysat was within walking distance of Hillary's street. Maybe in exchange for not having to drive Marybeth home, the woman she sat for would let Marybeth come earlier and leave earlier on Saturday afternoons. Then she could hitch a ride home with Peter from Hillary's.

Instead of being fun, the Saturday afternoon moviemaking sessions turned out to be an excuse for mischief. Marybeth was disgusted when she saw the first roll of film they had shot. It showed Hillary and Peter and another boy painting a yellow stripe around the car of a teacher no one liked. Then, apparently from some hiding place, they filmed the teacher's reaction when he discovered his car had been defaced.

On the way home, Marybeth said, "Peter, what was so funny about messing up that car? How could you do it?"

"Why are you always such a drag?" Peter said. "The paint comes right off with a little turpentine."

"And takes the finish with it, I'll bet."

"No. And anyway it wasn't a new car."

After a few weeks, the woman Marybeth babysat for complained of the change in hours. Marybeth gave up the movie-making sessions without regret. It was enough that she still went faithfully to the weekly parties with Peter even though she wandered through them like a lost soul. She kept hoping the newness of Hillary and her group would lose its appeal and Peter would be hers again. Sometimes he was still there for her when they were alone together. They weren't alone much though. Even the after-school phone calls had stopped entirely.

One afternoon Marybeth was riding her bike home from a quick run to the supermarket. She saw two people riding a motorcycle on the dusty tracks of an empty field. The person on the rear of the bike had on a curled-brim hat like the one she'd given Peter. She stopped pedaling to stare. It was Peter and Hillary. Hillary was wearing the hat. Pain tore through Marybeth. She pedaled home in a hurry, unable to speak to them. That evening she called Peter up and asked him to come over. She had taken enough. Now she was going to have it out with him.

She led him up to her bedroom for privacy, leaving the door open as she had promised Doris she always would if she brought Peter upstairs.

"Boy, am I tired," he said flopping on her bed. "I spent the whole afternoon trail-riding. If I don't get that bike on the road pretty soon, it's going to drive me crazy. But my marks should be okay this quarter. Grandpa should be satisfied."

All the beginnings in her head collapsed and the question exploded out of her. "What was Hillary doing wearing the hat I gave you?"

"What?"

"You told me you left that hat up in New Hampshire, Peter. How come Hillary was riding on the back of your bike wearing it this afternoon?"

He frowned at her, and then he lied. She could see

91

the lie in the vagueness of his eyes. "That wasn't your hat."

"Peter!"

"What?"

"Why did you tell me you left it in New Hampshire?"

"Because . . ." He sat up and rubbed his cheek thinking. Finally he admitted, "Because I felt dumb wearing it, Marybeth. My grandmother said I looked like a cowboy in it, and I didn't want to go around wearing it in public, and I didn't want to hurt your feelings."

"Then why did you say you liked it when you saw it?"

"I didn't think you were going to go out and buy it for me. All I did was admire it. I didn't say I wanted to own it."

"Oh."

"But, Marybeth, look—I'm sorry. Look, Hillary likes it a lot. She wants me to sell it to her."

"Go ahead."

"You don't care?"

"Why should I care? It's your hat."

"Maybe I'll—Marybeth, what's the matter with you now? You look sick."

"I don't like Hillary all that much, Peter. I don't like going around with her crowd."

"Yeah, I guessed you felt that way."

"Well, how do you feel about her?"

"I like her."

"Why?"

"I don't know. She's always got something going on. Things were getting kind of dull around here before Hillary came."

"Not for me they weren't dull."

"No? Look at all the parties we go to now. I mean, it's better for us not to be so stuck with each other."

"Is it?"

"You know what I mean. I mean, I'm not after you all the time like before. I've got other things to do so I don't think about trying to—you know, get you in bed with me."

"Is that all I meant to you?"

"Oh, come on."

"I asked you something, Peter. Is that all I meant? Don't we really love each other? Or were you only interested in getting me to have sex with you?" The words sounded so ugly in her own ears. She turned her back on him so that he wouldn't see the tears in her eyes. Weak—being sensitive was weak according to Hillary, something to mock. Well, she wasn't weak.

"I still love you, Marybeth. All I'm saying is it's nice we have something else to think about, that's all."

"I thought we had a lot to think about."

"Yeah, and it was driving me crazy."

"I don't mean that. You're back to sex again. It's not just sex, Peter."

"It sure isn't."

She got angry. Was sex more important to him than their caring for each other? "All right, then what would happen if I let you get to home base, then what?"

"Then what? What do you mean?"

"Then would you be satisfied?"

"Sure, it would make a difference."

"I mean, would you still want someone else to keep you from being bored?"

"How do I know? Look, you know I love you. Isn't that enough?"

Finally he was saying what she wanted to hear. She thrust out her arms blindly and felt his body press against hers, his hard, strong bones against all her soft, giving flesh. It felt so good in his arms. It felt so right.

"You're all the world to me, Peter," she said, and buried her uneasiness in a kiss that reaffirmed their oneness.

"I don't like Peter anymore," Lily complained in the middle of a TV commercial one evening in early December.

"Why don't you like him?"

"He never spends time with me anymore. He used to talk to me when you were getting ready or just sometimes when I met him outside, but now he's always too busy."

Marybeth shrugged. She couldn't do anything about that. The confrontation that she thought would change everything had had no effect at all. Peter was still running with Hillary's group while she watched from the sidelines.

The phone rang. Marybeth frowned as she went to answer it. Once she would have smiled.

"Hey, Marybeth," Peter said. "It turns out I'm not going to be around this weekend. Gotta go visit some relatives up at Blue Mountain Lake. Maybe get a chance to use my cross-country skis too. There's snow up there."

"I didn't know you had any relatives up at Blue Mountain Lake."

"Well, they don't live there. They're just visiting." His voice had an uneasy edge. Maybe he feels guilty about deserting me at such short notice, she thought. It was Friday night after all.

"Okay," she said. "I'm glad you'll get a chance to ski. Have fun."

"I'll miss you."

"You know I'll miss you," she said softly and waited, but he didn't seem to have anything else to say to her. She wondered if his grandparents were making him go with them the way they usually made him do anything, by bribing him with something he wanted.

"Okay," he said. "Take care now," and he hung up.

She put the receiver down, wishing she had thought to ask him why he hadn't told her about the visit sooner. Maybe his grandparents again. Well, she'd have time to catch up with her schoolwork, and she could spend Saturday night with the Frazier kids. The odd hour now and then that she had visited with them had been peculiarly unsatisfying in the past months. The children seemed subdued. They had lost their liveliness while their aunt had turned out to be a talkative, company-hungry person. She behaved, in fact, as if Marybeth's visits were for her benefit and rarely left Marybeth and the children alone together. It was hard to pay attention to Lise and Eric while politely listening to Florence's monologues. Florence was a complainer. True, she'd had a life worth complaining about, according to Doris, who'd had coffee with Florence a few times. Not only had she nursed her parents until they died, but she had moved in to take of Garth for a while after his mother's suicide when he was a boy. Garth had been the youngest in his family. But when Garth's father sank into alcoholism, Florence left to go as companion to an elderly woman in Florida. "He was a mean drunk," Florence said of Garth's father. "The only one who could handle him was the kid. Garth was a quiet kid, but gutsy, you know? I was scared to be alone in the house with the old man myself." Marybeth tried to imagine Garth as a kid dealing with a father who drank and a mother who committed suicide. Then he had married at twenty, probably because he was starved for love, and Laura had been so beautiful. It must have been heaven for him at first, but Marybeth remembered the bitterness she had sensed between them. He couldn't have been happy for too long. Poor Garth, Marybeth thought.

In her more cheerful moments, Florence liked to talk about Florida. Once in Marybeth's hearing, she told Doris she wanted to move back down there, get herself a trailer and have her own place for once.

"Maybe Laura will come back soon and you can go," Doris said.

"Her? She'll never be back," Florence answered. "She just sent word to him she was getting herself a divorce in Arizona or New Mexico or someplace like that. Told him all she wanted was her freedom and he could have custody of the kids."

"I can't see how a woman does that," Doris said. "Just walks out and never sees her kids again. I couldn't of done it, I'll tell you, even if I wanted to, which I didn't. My kids mean more to me than any freedom I could of had."

At home that night, Marybeth had reminded her mother of what she had said to Florence. "Did you really mean that, Mama, about how much we mean to you?"

"Sure I did." Doris gave Marybeth a clumsy kiss. "Don't you know how I feel about you without me having to tell you?"

Marybeth had laughed and returned the kiss, rubbing her cheek against her prickly mother with affection. The truth was she did know somehow. She had always felt that beneath Doris's griping there was abiding love.

As she planned, after supper Saturday night, Marybeth asked Lily if she wanted to go visit Lise and Eric. Lily shut off the TV immediately, always ready to go anywhere with Marybeth. They put on their winter jackets against the December chill. Yesterday two inches of snow had fallen, but they had shoveled it off their driveway, and it had pretty well melted off the road, so they didn't bother with boots. Though it was only six o'clock, the world outside was a black slate written over with smudges of snow and the traced outlines of rooftops and trees. Marybeth pointed out the evening star shining low in the sky.

"Hurry up, Marybeth," Lily said. "I'm cold. You should be too. I don't know why you didn't let Mama give you money for a new jacket. That's never going to keep you warm—the one you're wearing."

"I'll get another one when they have the clothing sale at the church."

"That won't be till next spring. You'll freeze to death in the meantime."

"Don't worry, Lily, I've got my love to keep me warm."

"Your love's in Blue Mountain Lake."

"No, it's not. It's right here." She put her hand over her heart and rapped on the door with the other hand.

Florence filled the doorway completely. "Well, Marybeth Mason! Your mother coming over?"

"No, she's working. Is it all right if we visit the kids?"

"Why not? We could use some company around here."

She stepped aside, and they walked into a living room that looked as if it hadn't been vacuumed and dusted since the summer. Marybeth tried not to notice, but Lily was frowning as she looked around. "The place is kind of messy," Florence said. "The kids—you just can't keep up with a place when there's little kids around. I just didn't get around to cleaning up this morning, not that that's my job, but there's no one else here to do it, so that leaves me elected cleaning woman along with every other job around here."

"Where are the kids?" Marybeth asked.

"Up in their room. I sent them up after dinner. I've gotta have some time to myself, but I can't just take off and go bar-hopping when I feel like it like my nephew does—just takes off and leaves me watching his kids like it's my duty or something. I said to him, 'Who works six days a week anymore?' Nobody. You don't find nobody will work those kind of hours—twenty-four hours a day, six days a week, except a poor relation like me who's got no choice. But get him to see that! Get him to see that I gotta have more than a couple of evenings a week off and Sundays. That man's blind to any needs but his own. Sit down, why don't you? I'll make you a cup of coffee."

"No, thank you," Marybeth said. "We'll go upstairs and play with the kids for a while."

"Well, they certainly don't deserve to get visitors the way they were rampaging around here today spilling everything in sight and not doing a thing I told them. It's hard, let me tell you, picking up the pieces in a broken home like this, and I'm not so strong as I used to be." She shook her head sadly at herself, and then looked at Marybeth and Lily, who stood waiting politely for her to release them. "Tell you what, I'll let the kids come downstairs for a half an hour. Then you can put them to bed for me, if you want."

"Yes, fine," Marybeth said. Lily said absolutely nothing, but Marybeth knew she wasn't liking Florence much.

Florence moved ponderously to the foot of the stairs and called, "Lise! You and your brother come downstairs *now!*"

Lily shrank away from the trumpeting voice. Marybeth winced. The door at the top of the stairs opened a crack. "We didn't do nothing!" Lise squeaked.

"Lise, it's Marybeth. Come on down and say hello," Marybeth called.

At once the door flew open and Lise came racing downstairs with arms wide and her stringy blond hair making a sail behind her. She wrapped herself around Marybeth as tightly as if she planned never to let her go. "Where's Eric?" Marybeth asked.

"Here he comes," Florence said. "That child! He acts dopier every day. Look at him!"

Marybeth looked at Eric now cringing against the wall on the top step. The steps had been covered with treads since the accident, but Eric seemed reluctant to come down them.

"Can't climb downstairs alone. Crawls around sometimes like he's still a baby, and he don't talk. You'd think a two-year-old could talk at least."

"Eric walks and talks fine," Marybeth said. "Maybe the fall he took down the stairs set him back, or it could be he misses his mommy, or . . . Eric, it's Marybeth and Lily. We came to see you." She unclamped Lise from her waist and went up the stairs to carry Eric down in her arms.

"I'm so glad Garth covered the steps," Marybeth said.

"That's the only thing he's done around this house," Florence said. "Lets the place go to wrack and ruin. He's never home. Says he has to work two jobs, but I wonder. If he doesn't have time to take care of his own children, then he ought to put them in foster care. That would be the best thing."

Marybeth set Eric down on the couch. He had lain limply against her and showed no particular interest in her. She thought he weighed less than he had in the summer. Certainly his energy was gone. Lise climbed onto the couch and took hold of Marybeth's arm and rubbed her cheek against it.

"Have the children been sick?" Marybeth asked. They looked sickly.

"Oh, they're always running something. It's this winter weather. Heaven knows what it's going to be like come January and February. I'm going to go out of my mind if I have to be stuck in the house all winter with these two."

Marybeth shut her ears against the sound of Florence's complaining voice. "Remember the song I taught you about the spider, Eric?" she asked the lethargic little boy. He shook his head no. "Want me to sing it again?" He just looked up at Marybeth. She felt her heart squeeze at the hopelessness of his expression. "Lise, you remember that song about the spider, don't you?"

"A little."

"Okay. Let's do it together for Eric. Itsy bitsy spider went up the water spout . . ." She made the motions of hands climbing and watched to see that Lise followed suit. "Down came the rain and—"

"Washed the spider out," Lise said.

"Out came the sun and—"

"Dried up all the rain," Lise said.

"And itsy bitsy spider went—"

"Up the spout again," said Eric clearly.

"There you go!" Marybeth applauded them. "That's good. Let's see; what else do we know?"

"Your mother say when she was coming over here?" Florence asked, interrupting as if Marybeth's doings with Lise and Eric didn't count for anything.

"No," Marybeth said. "She didn't say."

"Your mother's okay. She understands at least what it's like. She's another one who's had her hard knocks

100

like me. And she's a decent neighbor at least, not like the others around here. You could be dead before they'd notice you."

"Well, they're mostly older, retired people here on the bluff," Marybeth said. "Mr. Belladuci next door to you is a really nice man, but he's deaf, and then there's—"

"Just what I need!" Florence interrupted her again. "Living amongst a bunch of senior citizens with one foot in the grave. But like your mother says, when you don't have the education or no one to take care of you, you take whatever kind of job you can get just so you don't have to go on welfare. And believe me, the jobs that get offered aren't going to be anything but crap, the kind of work nobody else will do."

"Taking care of Eric and Lise seems like a good job to me," Marybeth said firmly. "I enjoyed it this summer."

"Oh yeah, sure, for you, playing mommy for a week or two is fun. You got young legs and nothing to worry about. Yeah, sure if I was your age, I wouldn't mind picking up some spending money that way. But you're not going to want to spend your life babysitting, are you?"

"Maybe," Marybeth said stubbornly. "I like children very much."

"Oh yeah? Well, kid, I'll tell you what. You just move in here with Garth and the kids and take over for me. Believe me, I'd be grateful. I don't know how much more of this job I can take. Trying to keep this place clean and chase after two little kids all day long—and do you think he appreciates what I'm doing for him? Not him. Mr. high and mighty, barely has a word to say to me, and the look on him—couldn't crack a smile if you paid him."

"Are we going to read the kids a bedtime story now, Marybeth?" Lily asked pointedly.

"Yes, that's a good idea," Marybeth said. "Have they had their baths yet?" It was obvious they hadn't.

"Not today, I decided it was too cold in the house. They just got over being sick, you know, but it's okay with me if you want to give them a bath. Tell you what, you get the kids to bed and come down, and we'll have a cup of coffee and a nice chat." She barely waited for Marybeth's agreement before flicking on the television that had been moved from the children's room to the living room.

Alone with the children in the steamy bathroom, Marybeth and Lily stretched bathtime out with songs and games and jokes. Even Eric cheered up and laughed a little. While Lily rocked Eric to sleep, singing in her tiny voice to him, Marybeth read a bedtime story to Lise, who tried hard to stay awake. Halfway through the story, the little girl's eyes closed.

"Do we have to go downstairs now?" Lily whispered. "I hate that lady."

"I could say we have to leave now," Marybeth said.

"Do that. I don't want to drink her coffee. She might put poison in it."

"Lily, don't be silly." But Marybeth was relieved when Florence accepted her excuse that they had to go because their mother would be nervous if she called home to check on them and they weren't there.

"Come again soon, why don't you?" Florence said, staring at the movie she was watching, allowing them to let themselves out.

How could Garth leave his children with a woman like that, Marybeth wondered. Maybe he didn't realize how bad Florence was with the kids. Marybeth thought of Eric's listlessness and fragility. She'd better have a talk with Garth. Surely there had to be a better arrangement for his children than to leave them in the hands of such an unloving woman.

Sunday as Marybeth was copying over her composition to hand in to her English teacher, Lily put her chin on Marybeth's shoulder. "You got me in trouble, Marybeth."

"I did? How?"

"You said they went away for the weekend, so I went for a walk around the Josselyns' house, and Mr. Josselyn was right there pruning a tree, and he asked me what I was doing on his property."

"What were you doing?"

"Nothing. I just like to go there so I can pretend I live there. It's such a fancy house."

"He wasn't nasty to you, was he?"

"No, but I was embarrassed."

"Maybe they got back from Blue Mountain Lake early. Wouldn't that be nice?" Marybeth said. "I'm going to call and ask Peter to come over and eat some of those cookies we baked."

"Good. Tell him his grandfather's mean."

Marybeth finished her copying quickly, spurred by the promise of seeing Peter after all. She dialed his number, hoping he, and not one of his grandparents would answer, but no luck. Mrs. Josselyn picked up the phone, and in a quavering voice as insubstantial as the old woman herself, asked, "Who is it?"

"Hi, this is Marybeth Mason. May I speak to Peter, please?"

"Who's there?"

"Marybeth Mason, Peter's friend from down the road?" She grimaced hoping Mrs. Josselyn didn't say, as she once had, that in her day nice girls didn't call up boys and bother them.

"Peter's gone," Mrs. Josselyn said. "He went away for the weekend."

"Oh, I thought he'd come home."

"That girl he went with said not to expect him until this evening. She said they were going to eat supper on the way back."

"I see. . . . Thank you," Marybeth said and hung up. He was with Hillary then. He had lied. He had said he was going to visit relatives when he was really going somewhere with Hillary. Her mind tumbled pebbles of unhappy thoughts, but couldn't smooth away their sharp edges.

"What's the matter, Marybeth? Is Peter coming?" Lily asked.

"Don't talk to me, Lily. I've got to be alone." She grabbed her jacket and ran out of the house and down the road until she was breathless. Then she slowed and zipped up the jacket while she made her way across yards to a point on the bluff where she could see the river. It flowed below her, black and cold as her thoughts. No ice on it yet except a few feet out along the banks and where the black, licorice ice was frozen over rock ledges. She stood staring at the ominous water. Why had she ever thought it was beautiful here? Why did she love Peter, who lied to her? Could she stop loving him if she had to? And if she couldn't stop loving him, if he deserted her finally altogether, what would happen to her then? The only answer in the black winter stillness was one for which she wasn't ready.

Chapter 8

She waited all Sunday evening for the phone to ring, and went to bed at eleven still not having heard from him. She wasn't surprised. His grandmother might not have told him about her call or he might have gotten in very late. On the other hand, he could have been reluctant to have it out with her. Monday morning she went to the bus stop ready to confront him. He wasn't there. She hunched her shoulders in her too-thin jacket against the wind tearing across the bleak fields and rehearsed the conversation they might have had. "Have a good time this weekend, Peter?" she would have asked, and when he answered, she would say, "I don't care what you do, but please don't ever lie to me."

In her homeroom an acquaintance asked, "What's wrong, Marybeth?"

"Nothing."

"You look as if something bad happened to you," the girl said.

Marybeth tried to change her expression, but she couldn't. Let people know then. Let Peter see it on her face. She wouldn't say anything to him. He would see how angry he'd made her and approach *her* to explain what he had done and why. If he loved her as he'd said he did, he would come to her. She would wait until he did.

At lunch time she took herself and her tray to the empty end of a half-filled table. She had never had to eat alone in her entire school life, but she could do that too if she had to.

"Is anyone sitting here?" The girl stood poised to move right by if Marybeth said yes.

"Nobody unless you'd like to," Marybeth said. The girl settled into the seat opposite Marybeth, tossing her waist-length braid of dark red hair back over her shoulder. She smiled at Marybeth from an earnest, freckled face, which Marybeth recognized.

"I remember you," Marybeth said. "Weren't you at the pool party this September?"

"You've got a good memory. Most people don't remember someone they just meet once like that. I wouldn't of remembered you except I was jealous of you."

"Of me?"

"Um hum. You had a boy with you. That made me jealous."

Marybeth sighed. The girl's honesty was appealing, but she couldn't talk to a stranger about Peter. "Maybe you wouldn't be jealous if you knew how complicated having a boyfriend can get."

The girl nodded. "My name's Melody."

"What a pretty name!"

"I think it's stupid."

"Really? I'll call you Mel then. My name's Marybeth Mason."

"Hi. Listen, this Saturday for a change I don't have a swim meet in the morning. Would you want to meet me at the mall and go window-shopping? Or do you have to see your boyfriend?"

"No. That would be fun—if I can get to the mall somehow. Give me your phone number and I'll call you Friday."

Mel's face lit up. She looked as if she hadn't expected Marybeth to say yes at all. Marybeth guessed Mel had been friend-hunting for a long time. It was funny how hard it could be to make friends if you were just the least bit different from the in-group. Probably Mel was just a shade too earnest. A swimmer—Marybeth wondered what they would have to talk about, but she didn't doubt she could find something. She always did.

"If you can't get to the mall, I'll come pick you up," Mel said. "If Mother lets me borrow her car."

"You drive? That's great."

"Don't you?"

"Not me." Marybeth laughed. She hadn't even considered learning how to drive yet.

Monday night he didn't call. She resisted the telephone as if it were a deadly sin to touch it. He would come to her. He had to come to her.

"What's the matter with you, Marybeth?" Doris asked.

"Nothing!" Marybeth cried. "Why can't you just leave me alone?"

Tuesday morning he was standing at the bus stop, and he asked, as if nothing had happened, "Why didn't you call me last night? Didn't you notice I wasn't in school?" His stuffed-up nose and blunted voice explained yesterday's non-appearance.

"For all I knew, you could still be up at Blue Mountain Lake."

"What are you mad about?"

"Why did you lie to me, Peter?"

"Lie about what?" He sounded so innocent that she got even angrier.

"About this weekend. You said you were going to visit a relative."

"I do have a relative in Blue Mountain Lake." He stopped to sneeze and dug out a tissue. "He's a cousin. I called him."

"Peter!"

"You don't believe me? Ask my grandparents then. They'll tell you."

"But you said you were going with your grandparents."

"I never said any such thing."

"Well, you let me think they were taking you, and really you were going up there with Hillary."

"I didn't tell you about Hillary because I didn't want you to be mad at me. You're already jealous of her."

"Well, don't I have reason to be?"

"No. I don't know what's got into you, Marybeth. You never used to be so possessive." He was quoting Hillary again.

"I'm not possessive. I know I don't own you. You can go do what you want with anybody—just tell me is all I ask. Don't lie to me."

"I didn't lie."

"Peter, there's no sense arguing about it."

"You're the one who's arguing."

"I'm not."

"Look, I told you all it was. I didn't want you to be mad at me. I'm sorry. Are you going to forgive me?" He looked so puppy-dog pathetic, she relented.

"You ought to at least zip your jacket when you've got a cold," she said.

"I hate it when you're mad at me, Marybeth."

"You're such a rat," she said weakly.

"Hillary's fun to be with as a friend," he said. "But you're my girl. You know that."

She smiled, blind to anything but the sound of his coaxing voice.

"Look," he said, and took her hand. In the snow he had traced a heart with the toe of his boot. Now he drew their initials inside the heart. "There we are," he said.

"What about when the snow melts?"

"Someday I'll get you a ring," he promised.

"Oh, Peter! I thought you didn't love me anymore," she confessed.

"What would you do if I didn't?" He wrapped his arms around her, resting his chin on her head.

"I don't know. Throw myself in the river or find another guy—one or the other."

"I'll never stop loving you, Marybeth."

And she believed him.

That night her mother was working at the diner and Lily was invited to a birthday party. Lily was thrilled that she had been invited, and besides the girl's mother was taking them all to see a movie about the life of a singer Lily idolized. When the car horn summoned her, she rushed out, listing awkwardly, her face bright with joy. Peter passed her on his way in as she was leaving. Marybeth held her breath, but Lily didn't even look back. She was probably too excited to realize that Marybeth and Peter were going to be alone in the house together for the first time. Peter shucked his coat in the living room and said, "Let's go up to your bedroom."

"What for?" Marybeth asked. "We have the whole house to ourselves. Do you want to watch television? Or I could turn on the radio and we could dance." But even as she tried to make it all sound ordinary, her heart was thrumming in her ears.

"Marybeth, let's go up to your room now."

"But Peter, if something happens—"

"Don't worry. I've come prepared."

It was as if she had become a robot under his control. She had to do as he said. She climbed the stairs, out of step with the fast beat of her heart, and walked stiffly into her bedroom. He never hesitated. He began to undress her as if she had no choice but to let him, to make love, to lie down on her bed and embrace his naked body, to move to the heated rhythms that his fingers found in her and his lips enticed and the touching of their bare skin created.

Afterward she couldn't pinpoint the moment when she should have said no. On the stairs it had already been too late. Perhaps it had been the moment when she let Lily go out the front door and allowed Peter to come on in anyway. It didn't matter, she decided. The thing was done. She belonged to Peter utterly now, not only her feelings, but her body too. She had given him the best proof she could of how much he meant to her.

Chapter 9

All week Marybeth watched for changes. Against the warnings of her mother and Sunday School teachers, she had given up her virginity. She kept expecting to feel guilty at the least, but she felt nothing, not even when she kissed Lily and her mother good morning. Surely then she should feel soiled, but she didn't. It puzzled her, this lack of reaction to something that should mean so much. After all, virginity could only be lost once, and she had lost it and she wasn't married and that was a sin no doubt, but she didn't feel sinful, just happy. If anything, she felt more loving. Peter was more loving too. He had never behaved as tenderly toward her.

She only realized what had changed that Friday when she remembered she was supposed to call Melody about their meeting at the mall. Marybeth didn't feel like calling. She was a woman now and would no longer have anything in common with an inexperienced girl like Mel. She considered making an excuse to cancel their appointment, but knew it would hurt the girl's feelings. She was about to dial when Lily ushered Lise into their kitchen.

"Marybeth, look at Lise's arm," Lily said.

"Hi, Lise. How are you doing?" Marybeth asked cheerily.

"Look at her arm," Lily urged.

Lise stood holding her left arm with her right hand, hunching her shoulder awkwardly. "It hurts," Lise said.

Marybeth touched the arm lightly, but as soon as she tried to move it, Lise screamed with pain. "It could be broken," Marybeth said. "We better tell Florence to take Lise to the doctor."

"I already told her," Lily said. "She says Lise's just whining."

Marybeth put her arm around Lise's good side and let the child lean against her. "How did your arm get hurt, Lise?" Marybeth asked.

"She shoved me."

"Who?"

"Aunt Florence. I didn't do nothing. She just shoved me across the room."

"I'll call Garth," Marybeth said.

"You better," Lily agreed.

"Where's Eric?" Marybeth asked.

"He's asleep," Lise said.

"Taking a nap?"

Lise shrugged her good shoulder. Her face looked parched. "Eric's always asleep," Lise said.

Marybeth got the telephone book and looked up the number of the garage where Garth worked. When she told him about the arm and that Lily said his aunt wouldn't take Lise to the doctor, he said, "I'll get there as fast as I can. Can you stay with Lise?"

The hospital emergency room looked the same as it had last summer when they had brought Eric after he fell down the stairs. The washable plastic and chrome chairs and scuffed tile floor, even the magazines with the torn covers, were the same.

"Lise says Florence shoved her," Marybeth said to Garth.

"Why was she mad at you, Lise?" Garth asked, looking down at the wan child in his lap.

"I got in her way," Lise said.

Garth nodded. "How long's Eric been sleeping, Lise?"

"I don't know."

"All day?"

"No."

"Since breakfast?"

"I can't tell you, Daddy."

"Why not?"

"I'm afraid. She said I better not tell you."

"What does she do to Eric?" Marybeth asked in horror.

"Dopes him so he'll sleep and she won't have to bother with him."

"And you let her do that?"

112

"I just began to suspect yesterday. Don't get upset, Marybeth. She's going. As soon as we get home, she's leaving my house." A tremor of anger went through him. "I don't know what I'm going to do about the kids though. I'm holding down two jobs so I can afford to pay someone to take care of them. I don't have any spare time to look for another sitter. But I'll have to find it somehow. I'll have to stay home and—"

"Don't worry, Garth. I'll take care of the kids until you find someone you can trust."

"You've got to go to school."

"A few days won't make any difference."

"I couldn't ask you to cut school."

"Why not? This is an emergency. Don't worry. You get that awful woman out of the house, and as soon as she's gone, I'll come."

"Your mother's going to object, and I couldn't blame her. It isn't right. This isn't your problem."

"Mother will understand. Look, do you think I could go to school worrying about who was taking care of the kids? I just wish I'd watched her closer."

A nurse called Lise's name and Garth carried her into one of the examining rooms leaving Marybeth to wait. Marybeth thought of Florence complaining that Garth was running around drinking at bars, enjoying himself while she was stuck taking care of the kids. Two jobs! No wonder the poor man looked as if he'd aged years since Marybeth saw him last. How did he stand it? Anger surged through her as she thought of Lise trapped with that woman all these months. She should have spent more time over there.

When she thought Doris might be home, Marybeth called and explained where she was and why.

"Oh, my God!" Doris said. "And Eric's home alone with her? I'll tell you what. I'll go over there and talk to Florence like I'm visiting until Garth gets back, and you're right, helping out there is more important than school right now. But maybe I can do something about finding someone to take care of his kids. A woman I work with has a mother. I'll see. Those poor tykes!"

Lise showed Marybeth her new cast proudly. "The nurse signed it," she said. "You want to sign it, Marybeth?"

"Sure I do," Marybeth said, "and I'll draw you a picture on your cast with a Magic Marker. Would you like that, Lise?"

In the car going home Marybeth told Garth what her mother had said about helping find a woman who would be good for the kids, and about permitting Marybeth to stay until someone could be found.

"Whenever things get really bad," he said, "the Masons come to the rescue. I'm lucky with my neighbors at least. I wish I could do something in return."

"Just keep the compliments rolling in. We like to hear how nice we are."

"You're nice. You're wonderful. You're beautiful," Garth said looking at Marybeth with an odd expression that she had never seen before.

The lines of tension that lifted from his face during the short car ride, set back in when he parked in his driveway. "She'll start packing tonight," he said. "And I'll drive her to the bus station in the morning."

"Call me as soon as you're ready to leave tomorrow then, and I'll come right over," Marybeth said.

"Aren't you going to draw a flower on my cast like you said?" Lise asked.

"I will tomorrow morning, Lise. Okay?"

In the morning Marybeth joined her mother at the kitchen table, where she was drinking a cup of coffee and sneaking one of the cigarettes that she had stopped smoking a year ago. "Mama!"

"Just wanted to see if they still tasted the same," Doris said.

"And does it?"

"Yeah, unfortunately."

"You're not going to start again after you stopped for so long?"

"I'd lose weight if I did."

"And get lung cancer and die young."

"I can't die young. I'm old already."

"Mama, listen. If Peter calls, will you give him Garth's number and tell him what happened?"

"Yeah, sure. You and Peter made up, huh?"

"Made up? We weren't fighting."

"Weren't you? I thought sure something must be wrong. He wasn't calling you, and you weren't seeing him so much. I thought maybe you were getting over it."

"I'll never get over it. I love Peter."

"Yeah, sure! The first boy you ever noticed and you think it's love. Don't rush it, Marybeth. Get as much fun as you can out of your teen years. You'll regret it if you don't."

"Mama, didn't you ever hear about anybody being childhood sweethearts and staying married their whole lives?"

"Yeah, once in a blue moon. Oh, all right, it can happen. Sure, and you always have been a little woman even when you were five. I remember how you used to mother Lily. Sometimes I got jealous because you were better with her than I was. It came more natural to you. I sure was never a mother type. I was a little devil as a kid—wanted to be a boy in the worst way. I used to say I wanted to be a ball player when I grew up." She grinned. "I should of had sons. Of course, as things worked out, I'm better off. I had you." She kissed Marybeth lightly on the cheek, and

out of nowhere the thought came to Marybeth—
"What if I got pregnant?" Doris would probably never
forgive her. For the first time, Marybeth experienced
the guilt she had expected. Even if they had been
lucky this time, and the rubber Peter had used had
worked, she would have to make Peter understand
they couldn't take any more chances. A year and a half
until they graduated, eighteen months, a lot of weeks
and too many days.

After Florence left that morning, Marybeth took
over the Frazier household. She and Lise were building a house of blocks with Eric, who was laughing
again whenever he accidentally-on-purpose knocked a
pile down. Lise was annoyed with him for obstructing
progress, but Marybeth was so glad to see him
laughing that she would have constructed houses for
him to knock down all day long. Then the phone rang.

"Hi," Peter said. "I was looking for you last night. I
have something to give you."

"Did Mama explain about Lise's arm?"

"Yeah. How long are you going to have to be with
them?"

"Until Garth finds somebody else who'll take good
care of them."

"You sure get yourself into things, Marybeth. Don't
you want to know what I have for you?"

"What?"

"It's a present."

"What for? It's not Christmas yet."

"But I can't wait. Can I come over there?"

"Sure. We can play horsey. You give Lise a horsey
ride and I'll be Eric's horsey. Isn't that a good idea,
Eric?"

"Horsey?" Eric said, looking up at her, bright-eyed
with anticipation.

"Marybeth," Lise complained. "Eric keeps knock-

116

ing my house down. I don't want to play this any-more."

"We'll play something else," Marybeth said, and then to Peter, "Hurry up. I miss you."

Peter blew in five minutes later, with his jacket winged out in the wind behind him, looking so ador-able Marybeth had to grab and kiss him right away.

"Hey," he said. "Are we alone here?"

"No. Lise and Eric are here."

"I mean—no adults."

"You better not mean anything, Peter. Just because we were crazy once doesn't mean we're going to take chances like that again."

"Why not?"

"Because." He should know the becauses well enough, she thought, without having her go into them in detail.

"Marybeth, don't you want to see what I have for you?" he said.

"Sure I do. Where is it?"

"You find it." He stood there grinning with a glint in his eye that she understood all too well.

"Lise, Eric!" Marybeth called, thinking quickly. "My friend Peter's got a present for me and he's hiding it. Help me find it." She began tickling him until he doubled over to escape, yelling.

"No fair. Cut that out, Marybeth. You're not play-ing fair."

Marybeth shoved him onto the couch and Eric and Lise climbed aboard. The kids screamed with glee and poked at all his pockets. It was anything but the sexy search Peter had expected. Marybeth laughed, glad he was so ticklish. It was her best defense when he was pressing too hard.

"I sure hope my present isn't breakable," she said, giggling as the kids turned out his pockets.

117

The small, flat box was in his jeans pocket. In his socks and disarrayed clothes he sat cross-legged on the couch, watching her open it. "Soon as I saw it, I knew you'd like it," he said.

"Oh, Peter!" she exclaimed pressing her hands to her cheeks. The gold heart on a thin gold chain took her breath away. She couldn't help herself; she began to cry.

"Hey, that's not what you're supposed to do," he said. "You're supposed to try it on. It's real gold—outside anyway. Do you like it, Marybeth?"

"What a dumb question! It's just beautiful. But why did you—"

"Because I wanted to."

"Why?"

"So you have something that shows you how much I love you."

That was all she needed to hear. She burst into noisy tears. Lise and Eric thought something was wrong and began to cry too. "Don't cry," Marybeth instructed them between sobs, "Don't you cry. I'm just so happy." She spread wild, wet kisses among the three of them, and finally everyone calmed down enough for Peter to open the tiny clasp and close the chain around Marybeth's neck.

"There," he said. His lips met hers in a long, searching kiss that she knew would lead to a lovemaking she was not going to allow no matter how desire took hold of her. She pushed him away.

"No, absolutely no," she said.

"I hear you, but I don't hear you," he said. "Don't the kids have to take a nap or something?" He pressed against her, sliding his fingers up under her hair along the base of her skull. His lips insisted and her breasts ached for his touch.

"You've got—to stop—now!" She gasped and pulled away and ran out of the room to the bathroom, where she locked the door behind her.

"Hey, Marybeth, I thought you loved me," he complained outside.

"You go away, Peter," she said sadly. "You have to leave unless you're willing to play with the kids instead of with me." She had the momentary thought that it was hard enough to resist her own urges without having to be the one to control his as well, and the next thing he said annoyed her more.

"I don't want to spend my Saturday playing games with babies, Marybeth."

"Suit yourself. I'll see you then—tomorrow. Okay?" Garth would take over tomorrow.

"What about tonight?"

Saturday night, she thought. Saturday nights were sacred to their togetherness. "I can't. Unless you want to come over here and you promise to behave yourself. We could play Boggle or checkers or you could teach me backgammon."

"You're kidding! We've got a big party to go to tonight."

"I can't go. Garth has to work tonight."

"Let Lily stay with the kids."

"She's afraid to stay alone, 'specially in a strange house."

"Marybeth, it's not fair," he protested as if the party were really important.

"You'll just have to go without me." She hoped that would bring him to his senses.

He sighed. "I guess," he said.

She unlocked the door and stepped out of the bathroom. He sounded cooled down enough for it to be safe for her to come out. Was the party really so important to him that he would go without her? She touched the heart, which was already warm from her skin.

"Peter, if you came over here, it would be just like sitting around at my house after the kids are in bed."

"Who wants to just sit around on Saturday night? Anyways, I don't see why what's going on here is any of your business."

She looked at him wide-eyed. "Peter, Lise's arm was broken. The woman abused the kids. If you saw some kids being abused, wouldn't you step in and help them?"

"Well, sure, if I was the only one around. But he could get another babysitter for tonight, couldn't he? *You* could find some girl to substitute for you if you called around."

"Lise and Eric need someone they know right now. They've been through an awful experience. After all, their mother left them and then—Peter, *you* ought to understand."

"You're making too big a thing of it."

"How can you say that?"

"Okay, okay, so do your good deed if you've got to, but I'm not going to sit around playing kiddie games all day."

"So don't."

"Maybe I'll call up Hillary and ask her if she wants to go skiing."

"Go ahead."

"You don't care?"

"I don't own you, Peter."

"How come you're looking at me like that then?"

"Like what?"

"Like I hit you in the face or something."

She shrugged. "Thanks for the heart."

"Marybeth, I do love you, but I'm not going to do everything your way. You gotta understand that."

She shut her eyes against the tears. He kissed her eyelids gently, which started the tears flowing anyway. When she found a tissue in her pocket and wiped her cheeks dry, he was gone. Lise held her on one side and Eric patted her arm consolingly on the other. Marybeth touched the gold heart. He loved her. So what if he went skiing with Hillary. It would be okay. "Let's make some lunch," she said to the children.

Sunday afternoon Marybeth started apologizing as soon as she got in the door because she had forgotten to leave a note for Doris and Lily who had been out shopping for a Christmas tree. "I was just across the street, Mama. Garth called and asked me to come help him interview that lady you recommended. I was so surprised when he asked me. I couldn't believe it. But he said nobody knows more about taking care of his kids than I do. It made me feel so good."

"It's true," Doris said.

Marybeth blinked. Another compliment from her mother? Doris must be getting into the habit. "He's not much of a talker," Marybeth said. "I think that's the real reason he wanted me there. She and I did most of the talking while he listened. I think she's very nice, and the kids took to her right away. I sure hope it works out this time."

"If not, he'll find somebody else," Doris said. "There's two kinds of people, Marybeth—those that expect life to be easy and give up if it isn't, and those that don't expect a thing and don't ever stop trying. Garth is the kind who doesn't know how to quit."

"Like you," Marybeth said. Doris shrugged and

smiled. Marybeth touched her necklace thinking of Peter. He expected life to be easy. She knew that. But he was only sixteen, and boys of sixteen weren't usually as mature as girls were. Peter could turn out as steady and responsible as Garth Frazier. Probably at sixteen Garth had his mind set on having fun too. Or had he? Maybe that was when he was handling his alcoholic father. She wondered if he had ever had a chance to have fun.

"It's very pretty," Doris said, watching Marybeth finger her gold heart. "He couldn't wait to give you your Christmas present, huh? Looks like it cost enough. Well, he can afford it."

"Oh, Mama! Don't you think Peter works for his money just like anybody else? He's got that snow-blower he does driveways with."

"Yeah, and a handy allowance from his grandfather too, I'll bet."

"You never give him any credit." Her mother's attitude toward Peter always irritated Marybeth. Now she said, "I'm going to steam the creases out of the wool skirt for school tomorrow. Do you want me to press anything for you?"

She ironed, wondering why Peter hadn't called all day. She hoped he wasn't angry with her for not going with him last night. From his point of view, maybe he had a reason to be angry. Here he gave her this beautiful present and she wouldn't even go out with him. But that was silly. He must understand why she couldn't leave the children. Then why hadn't he called? She was considering calling him when the phone rang. She ran for it, smiling expectantly.

"Marybeth? This is Hillary. Now don't hang up. I have to talk to you."

Marybeth closed her eyes and stopped smiling. Hillary, not Peter. "Why should I hang up?"

"I just thought you might not want to talk to me. Have you spoken to Peter today?"

"No."

"Oh. . . . Well, I think it's important you and I keep an open communications link between us anyway."

"I don't know what you're talking about, Hillary."

"I mean to prevent any misunderstandings. I always think it's sad when relationships get fouled up just because of misunderstandings that could have been cleared up if people only talked to each other."

"I guess I'm dumb. I still don't understand what you're getting at."

"Peter."

"What about Peter?"

"Well, I know you know we spent the day together yesterday because he told me he told you."

"Yes."

"Just yes? I didn't think you'd be so permissive, Marybeth. Good for you. I'm impressed."

"Impressed by what?"

"That you can care about him the way you do and still not try to tie him to your apron strings."

"I'm not his mother."

"Aren't you? Sometimes I think he thinks you are the way he talks about you."

Marybeth was certain Peter didn't think of her as his mother, not the way he was always after her to make love. Hillary was just trying to stir up trouble. She wanted Peter for herself. That's all this phone call was.

"How come you're so quiet?" Hillary asked.

"You're the one who called me," Marybeth said.

"Well, I have to tell you something."

Marybeth waited.

"You're not going to like it. Are you listening? . . . Here goes. Peter says he's crazy about me."

"Does he?"

"You don't believe me?"

"No, I don't." She touched the heart, warm as love and hard as forever. She wasn't going to let Hillary upset her.

"All right. You think what you want, but I'm being open with you. Peter says he's wild about me and from now on we're going to be sharing him, Marybeth. From now on you better not count on getting invited to parties with him as a couple. My friends will invite him with me."

"Is that all you called up to tell me?"

"I also wanted to tell you that I care about him just as much as you do. You've got to understand that."

"You can't know how much I care about Peter."

"No, right. I can't. But I know you must care a lot or you wouldn't have gone all the way with him. You're a good church-going Catholic girl who wouldn't do that easily. Am I right?"

"I'm not Catholic." She was so shocked she hardly knew what she was saying. Peter wouldn't tell Hillary, would he? He wouldn't offer up their most intimate moments to Hillary.

Marybeth shivered with disgust as Hillary said, "Well, whatever religion. Anyway, I just wanted to be open with you. We're even, you and I . . . Last night I had sex with Peter too."

"I don't believe you," Marybeth said. She set the receiver back in place gently. When the phone rang again, she pressed the buttons down and didn't answer even though her mother, sitting in the living room watching television with Lily, called to ask her who it was. Marybeth stared at the flour canister, which had a powdering of flour over it that Lily should have wiped off. Had Hillary made up the story? Would she be that sneaky? It seemed possible except that Peter wouldn't do that to Marybeth. He wouldn't tell Hillary, and he wouldn't turn around and make love to her as if it didn't matter who—as if having sex was all that mattered to him.

Suddenly she couldn't stay in the house another minute. She cut through the living room and dashed out the front door, taking her coat but not stopping to put it on. She raced over the slippery, snow-banked lane in her houseslippers and through the ankle-deep snow on the Josselyns' property. She rang their front doorbell, something she hadn't dared do since Peter's grandmother answered the door and said, "Don't you have any shame?" when Marybeth asked for Peter.

Right now if anyone asked her that, she would say, "No, I don't." She loved him and her heart was splintering into slivers of doubt. Only he could bind it back together again. "Hillary was lying," he would say. "I don't love anyone but you."

Peter opened the door and looked surprised. "Marybeth, what's wrong? Why aren't you wearing your coat?"

"Come out. I've got to talk to you."

He had on work boots and jeans. He pulled on his jacket, helped her to put on hers, and called over his shoulder, "I'm going out for a while. Be back soon." Then he took Marybeth's hands and blew on them to warm them.

"You nut," he said. "What's the matter with you?" His voice curled around her, and his long-lash-fringed eyes were warm with concern.

"Peter, do you really love me?"

"You know I do. Is that what you came running through the snow without any shoes on to ask me? Hey, tell you what—Let's go get your boots and walk over to the road and hitchhike to the mall. I've been wanting a chocolate shake all day."

"Let's just walk. I have to talk to you."

"Something's really wrong, huh? Hey, you're not—no, you wouldn't know yet, would you?"

"Pregnant?" She looked at the soft contours of his lovable face. "Suppose I was pregnant, what would you do?"

He considered. "Well, first you'd have to go to a doctor to make sure."

"And then?"

"I don't know. I guess, we'd figure out a way to get rid of it."

"You mean an abortion?"

"Yeah."

All at once she felt the cold gripping her wet feet. Overhead the power line swayed in the wind. The world was silhouetted against the gray-blue evening sky. "I'd never get an abortion," she said surprised to find herself saying something so self-evident aloud.

"Marybeth, you're not pregnant. But if you were, you'd have to think about it. I mean, you're only sixteen."

"I'd go to a home for unwed mothers if Mama kicked me out of the house, and I would plan to keep the baby."

"Okay, sure, whatever you say."

"I thought you understood me, Peter. After all these years I'd think you would understand me better."

"I do understand you."

"Then you ought to know that's how I'd feel."

He kept his head down and his hands in his jacket pockets as he walked beside her. "I sure hope you're not pregnant," he said, "because I sure am not ready to be a father. I'm still getting yelled at for not remembering to put the garbage out. I'm a kid, for heaven's sake, and so are you."

"Then what are we doing going to bed together?"

"Oh, come on! Sex doesn't mean you've gotta get

married and have babies right off. I mean, what century are you living in?"

"Tell me what you mean when you say you love me?"

"I don't know what you want me to say. I just do."

"But what do you mean? Are we going to get married someday?"

"Maybe."

"Maybe? I'll tell you what I mean when I say love, and then you tell me."

"Okay."

"I mean you are all I need. I mean if there was just you and nobody else in the whole world, that would be enough for me. I want to be with you all the time and share everything with you, and if one of us had to die, I'd rather it was me." She paused considering whether she had said everything. "I guess that's it."

"That's pretty heavy." He looked downcast. A brown setter trotted by, head down, tail straight back, looking cold and in a hurry. A car turned into the lane from the highway, backed into a driveway and drove out the opposite way. The houses all showed lights though it was only five o'clock. Marybeth felt chilled now, not just her feet but all of her. Still she waited for him. They walked back toward her house. Finally he said very seriously,

"I guess when I say I love you, I'm talking about how I feel. It's a feeling, I mean, like love is just something inside me that I can feel sometimes. I don't know what else it means. Just I feel something special with you, and I like to be with you a lot, and I care about what happens to you, and mostly I wanna tell you when something happens to me." He hesitated. "That's about it, I guess." He looked at her as if to see if that was what she wanted.

Already, she had forgotten what he had said. It

seemed he had left too much out, but she couldn't remember what. "What about other girls?" she asked.

"I can still love you and be friends with other girls."

"What about sex then?"

"What do you mean?"

"If you have sex with a girl, that's more than friendship."

"Well, but—" He let his breath out while he tried to find his way out of that one. "See, sex and friendship are two different things, and they don't either of them have to have anything to do with love. I mean, you don't expect me not to have any sex until I'm married, Marybeth. Do you?"

He made it sound so unreasonable. She looked at him in the dark trying to see across the gulf of their difference. "But love means being faithful," she said.

He protested indignantly. "You can't have it both ways, Marybeth. It's not fair. You say you don't want to go all the way with me anymore. Well, okay, but you can't expect me to stifle myself until I'm married."

"Why not? I'm supposed to. Why can't you?"

"Oh, come on! You know that's not the way it works."

"Did you have a good time with Hillary yesterday?"

"Yeah. We went skiing."

"Is that all you did?"

"What do you mean?"

"Hillary called me this afternoon."

"Yeah, what about?"

"About what you and she did yesterday."

He didn't say anything. She could feel him trying to figure out what Hillary might have told her. She shivered violently, feeling raw with disgust at him and at herself for poking and probing at this wounded thing that had once been so beautiful. Inside her brain a worldly-wise voice began asking, "What did you expect of him?" He was a sixteen-year-old kid. Her loving didn't make him a man. Someday he would grow up—maybe. If she wanted him enough, she would wait until he had matured enough to love her back the way she loved him. And if she wasn't willing to wait, what would she have then? Nothing, a hopeless emptiness where all hope had been.

"We might as well go home," she said. "I'm freezing."

He didn't ask her anymore about what Hillary had told her. He seemed glad to drop the subject. They ran into her house, and he took her hands and kissed them. "Poor baby," he said. "We'd better get you warm. Best thing is to go take a hot bath. I'll turn on the water for you."

Lily and Doris came running and instantly Marybeth was a patient, able to stop thinking. She let go of herself and allowed them to take care of her. Doris yelled at her for running outside unprotected in this weather like a fool. Lily and Peter ran about trying things to warm her up. It wasn't until Marybeth was alone in the steamy bathroom that the feeling of loss overwhelmed her. She sat in the tub letting her tears drip into the water while her hands and feet stopped burning with cold and the water cooled slowly. She was sleepy when she went downstairs in her quilted robe. Peter was watching television with Lily and Doris. Marybeth sat down to wait until the program was over.

"You're not mad at me?" he asked when he kissed her goodnight at the door and she just stood there.

"No, I'm not mad at you."

He smiled then and left her. She went up to bed and went to sleep, too tired to think anymore. She'd have plenty of time to think if she was going to wait for him, plenty of time until he became a man.

Monday when she saw Melody's pigtail going down the corridor in school, she remembered. Oh my God, I forgot to call her! "Melody, wait up," she yelled.

The girl stopped and looked over her shoulder, but when she saw who it was, she kept walking. Marybeth pursued her and caught up with her in the girls' room.

"Melody, I can't tell you how sorry I am. I just completely forgot to call you. I had my hand on the phone, but then you won't believe what happened."

"I don't care. It doesn't matter." Her face was expressionless and she looked right at Marybeth who persisted.

"It does matter. I wanted to see you Saturday but—"

"I *said* it doesn't matter. I was too busy anyway."

"Well, how about next week? Would you like to come over Friday after school and sleep over at my house?"

"No, thank you."

"But—"

"I'm really too busy. My swim meets and all." She ended the discussion by stepping into a just vacated stall and shutting the door behind her. Marybeth felt sick. She had hurt Melody, been careless of her feelings. In her mind she saw Melody waiting and waiting for the phone to ring. Hadn't the girl as much as said she didn't have any friends and now Marybeth had rejected her too. No wonder Melody was bitter. Marybeth walked out of the girls' room depressed. She had failed in the one area in which she had confidence in her own ability—caring, being sensitive to another person's needs.

The river was locked in and still. Ice covered it from bank to bank, and snow transformed it into nothing more mysterious than a flat field between twin rock ledge walls and steep banks. She got no pleasure from the river in February. She had never gotten so little pleasure from daily living as she was getting now. She smiled when she remembered to, but the smile was automatic, a winter smile. She talked to people, but their answers didn't really interest her. She was frozen over with waiting.

"I told you not to put your faith in that boy," Doris scolded. "I told you he was nothing but a spoiled kid, but you always know better than your mother. Well, now you'll listen to me when I say the best thing a girl can do is prepare herself to make it on her own. You've got to get what there is out of life and the heck with expecting anything good out of men. Now I know you aren't impressed with your Aunt Janet. And I'm not saying her way is the only way, but at least she lives well, and she isn't beholden to anybody for her pleasures. Stop thinking about Peter, Marybeth. Think about what you're going to do with yourself after high school. Maybe you ought to get some nurse's training. Or, I know a dietitian who makes good money and says she likes her job."

She saw him with Hillary sometimes around the school or driving off on the motorcycle for which his grandfather had finally allowed him to get a license. Anger would jolt her when she saw him with Hillary, laughing, growing handsomer daily and more cool and self-confident while Marybeth felt herself shriveling in the cold of waiting. She couldn't force love out of him.

He treated her like an old friend, like an old lover, and he went out with other girls. Naturally he went out with other girls, she thought. He hadn't found the one who mattered more to him than any other yet. Suppose that girl turned out to be Hillary? Marybeth didn't believe it. Suppose he kept looking and Marybeth kept waiting, and he never claimed the river of love she had for him. She didn't believe that either. She thought it was just a matter of suffering through the waiting. She thought he would return to her.

Chapter 10

By spring Marybeth had taken to looking for omens. Walking with Lily down the lane, she saw a tiny wren trying to oust sparrows from the birdhouse on the Josselyns' property where it had nested the year before. If the wren succeeded, she told herself, Peter would lose interest in Hillary and return to her. Two days later she went back alone to look and the wren had indeed won, but that weekend Peter spent no time with her at all. Standing at the bus stop, she watched paper blowing across the road. If it reached the other side before a car ran over it, Peter would call that night. The paper escaped and Peter did call.

She knew it would mean a visit from him if she woke up to sunshine after six days of rain. Two days of sunshine passed without a sign of him. It didn't discourage her that the omens were as often wrong as right. She needed to believe in something. She needed a way to pass the time of her waiting. The omens were a game. When they promised good, she had something to look forward to. When they were discouraging, then she prepared against disappointment.

More and more her only contact with Peter was his cheery greeting when he passed her in the halls at school. Occasionally he needed a companion on spur-of-the-moment jaunts in the perky little car he had bought when he discovered that the motorcycle was nearly useless in the wintertime.

"You and Lily want to get some flowers, Marybeth? I know where there's forsythia bushes nobody owns."

He could spend a couple of hours with them, treat them to sundaes on the way home, talk earnestly about how he had enough talent at tennis so he should have joined the tennis team and maybe become a pro, and about the movie that Hillary's group had finally finished and how funny it was though not something they could exhibit publicly. He mentioned the trip to Alaska he was planning with an older fellow over summer vacation. He teased Lily about having a boyfriend, "Girl as pretty as you—what do you mean you don't have a boyfriend?" Sometimes he hugged and kissed Marybeth affectionately, but as if she were a friend, not the girl he loved. Then the next day he would be off to play tennis with Hillary or to pay endless visits to people in her social set, his social set now.

In school Peter behaved toward both Marybeth and Hillary with casual affection, but Marybeth never sat with them at lunch. She had found a niche for herself with a small group of girls who escaped being socially graded and boxed into place in the cafeteria by bringing their lunches to the Home Ec room where their very pregnant Home Ec teacher held sway. Mrs. Handy enjoyed having them gather snug around her to discuss family life and ways to save money and recipes and—sometimes—boys. For all of them there except Marybeth and Mrs. Handy, the knowledge of boys was only theoretical. Once Marybeth asked, "Why don't marriages last anymore in our society?"

"Why, lots of reasons," Mrs. Handy said. "Women are no longer dependent on men to support them so they don't have to stick out a bad marriage. And I guess the pace of life being faster causes disruptions in marriage as well as everywhere else."

"But isn't it important to have relationships that last?" Marybeth asked, yearning for an affirmation of her belief.

Mrs. Handy laughed the nervous laugh that meant she found a question awkward. Finally she said, "Nothing lasts these days. Everything's made to wear out fast and be replaced."

"Love and marriage shouldn't. The longer they last, the more beautiful they become," Marybeth said.

"I think you're right." Mrs. Handy looked at her sympathetically. "But things aren't always the way they should be, are they?"

Once in the supermarket, Marybeth saw Hillary and Peter walking hand in hand and her heart lurched. She turned into the next aisle, so faint she nearly knocked over a display of tuna fish. Even if she saw him unexpectedly when he was alone, the fact that she could no longer run to him and claim her place beside him left her breathless and disoriented.

Warm April days she climbed down to a jutting rock above the muddy river bank and stared at the torpid, greenish-brown water. If the branch, which was caught in that little pool behind the miniature dam, escaped, then Peter would return to her by summer. If the lone fisherman on the opposite bank caught something while she was watching—if the chipmunk reappeared . . . and the river moved on, its voice burbling with energy, flushed with spring promise, but she was fixed on the bank like a dead tree that spring would never touch again.

The Junior Prom was going to be a re-creation of a fifties' dance. It would be held at the second nicest country club in town. The girls were to wear long dresses. Her Home Ec room friends complained that it was disgusting to make the dance so expensive, that lots of kids couldn't afford to go. Why not hold it in the school gym as always and have everybody wear what they wanted? But Marybeth didn't care that the dance was undemocratic. She longed to wear a real gown and go to a dancing party like a fairy-tale Cinderella one night of her life.

"What do you think about holding the dance at the country club?" Peter had asked her.

"It should be nice."

"You'd like to go, huh?"

"Yes," she said.

"I don't know if it's really worth it, getting all dressed up like that. If I was going to go, I'd have to rent a fancy rig or something. I don't know." She held her breath hoping, and yet she wasn't surprised when he asked Hillary.

A boy Marybeth sometimes talked to in Social Studies invited her to the prom. She thanked him but said she didn't think she should go.

"Why didn't you say yes to him?" Lily asked.

"I just don't want to go with anyone else."

"But Peter's going out with other girls. Why can't you go out with other boys?"

"I just can't, Lily."

"I read an article that says the way to stop your boyfriend from taking you for granted is to go out with other guys. Why don't you make Peter jealous, Marybeth?"

"I just don't feel like going out with anyone else." She lacked enthusiasm for doing anything much. Even ordinary activities like going to church or working on the church bazaar were hard to force herself to do.

"You're getting awful lazy," Doris said when Marybeth hadn't gotten around to cleaning the bathroom.

"I'm sorry, Mama."

"Are you sick or something?"

"No. I just feel tired all the time."

"Spring fever," Doris said.

Finally Todd Mathus, who was very shy, got up the courage to ask Marybeth to go to a movie with him. She had always made an effort to be friendly to Todd just because of his painful shyness, and now she couldn't hurt him by saying no. Their Saturday night date was hard work for her. She had to keep the conversation going singlehandedly, and besides that, cover up the fact that it was a monologue so that he would go home feeling good about himself. She babbled cheerful nonsense nonstop except during the hour-and-a-half-long movie, which wasn't a long enough relief break. During the movie he put his arm around her. That, or just the fact that she had gone out with him, seemed to cinch it for Todd. He regarded her as his girlfriend. He left her at the door saying he would come by and see her the next afternoon. She put him off, and instantly his fragile confidence evaporated. She wound up feeling guilty that she had encouraged him at all. It seemed misleading to beckon him out of his shyness and then reject him. Seeing him withdraw into himself, she invited him impulsively to go to a church supper with her next weekend. But their relationship was never anything but a strain on her. In a few weeks she ran out of even silly topics of conversation.

"I guess we don't have much to say to each other," he said.

'I guess not," she agreed and was relieved when he slipped out of her life. Despite the article Lily had read, Peter hadn't seemed to care one way or the other, though he knew she was seeing Todd. And as for Todd's shyness, he withdrew right back into it, so she didn't feel she had done him any good either.

On the night of the prom, Marybeth crept out to the back of Garth's yard, where she could see both the river and the Josselyns' house. She watched the upstairs window until she saw Peter's light go out. Then she saw him striding around the house to the back, where he parked his car. All she could see of him at such a distance was the outline of his broad shoulders and slim waist in the white pants and fancy jacket. She closed her eyes after his car drove off, so tired she could barely drag herself home and upstairs to bed. She spent a lot of her time sleeping. It seemed lately she could not get enough sleep.

"It isn't normal," Doris said. "You've got to see a doctor, Marybeth. Maybe you're anemic or something. Janet says I should send you to a psychologist. Is that what it is? Are you still mooning around over that dumb kid down the road after all this time?"

"Mama, please don't nag me. I feel fine."

"You're not pregnant or anything, are you?"

"No," Marybeth said. "I'm not pregnant."

By the end of June when Marybeth went to the going-away party Peter was giving for himself before he took off for Alaska in a van with his male friend, Peter and Hillary were no longer going out with each other. Hillary was seeing a boy on the tennis team.

Peter didn't seem to care. He invited Hillary to his party too. Everyone was his friend. Marybeth stood watching him trying to get kids to use the volley ball net he'd set up. She had the strangest sensation of not being there. The person standing on the lawn in her sandals was a member of the party, but she herself was an observer. She had been observing from the sidelines for so long that that ghostly role seemed her real self.

"You aren't still gone on him, are you, Marybeth?" Hillary asked, coming up beside her.

Marybeth looked Hillary in the eye without answering.

"He's not worth it, you know," Hillary said.

"Isn't he?" Marybeth asked, indifferent to Hillary, who shrugged and walked away.

Later Peter found Marybeth rooted there and asked her, "What do you want me to bring you back from Alaska, baby doll? Want some mukluks? Want a walrus tusk?"

"A letter would be nice." She smiled at him.

"Oh, you know what a rotten letter writer I am. I'll send you a postcard if I get the time. . . . What are you going to do with yourself this summer?"

"Nothing much. Work probably. They may use me part time in the diner where my mother works."

"Well," he said, "I hope you have fun anyway. It's been a long time for us, hasn't it?" He squeezed her arm and moved back into the floating fragments of his party, leaving her to wonder what he meant. A long time. Yes, she thought, it had been a long time.

Chapter 11

The summer surprised Marybeth. With Peter gone and nothing to hope for until his return, everything worked out better than she expected. Her energy came back and her enjoyment of little things, like good weather and food and another person's happiness.

The day after her seventeenth birthday, Marybeth was asked to start working at the diner to fill in for a girl who was sick. "You're going to hate it," Doris assured her, but started teaching her how to hold a tray and who to steer clear of in the kitchen and how to remember which customer had ordered blue cheese dressing on his salad and which wanted the onions left off. Doris was so nervous over how her daughter would do that she nearly succeeded in shaking Marybeth's confidence, but not quite. Marybeth was an instant success. The customers liked her because of her cheerfulness. She was patient even with the fusspots and the indecisive ones. The other waitresses liked her because she was friendly, didn't get flustered easily and learned quickly. Even the hostess, who was everybody's enemy, seemed to take to Marybeth. The first few days Doris kept up her dire predictions. "You think it's a game now because it's new, but you wait. If you end up waiting tables full time all your life, you'll hate it soon enough."

Marybeth thought she probably never would mind the work so much as Doris did. It wasn't in her nature to mind things so much, but she didn't irritate her mother by arguing with her. Now at home, Doris chatted with Marybeth about the snippy ways of the hostess and the chef's notorious bad temper and the soap-opera love life of another waitress, as if their relationship had changed, and Marybeth had become a friend. Lily noticed and was disgruntled.

"Don't you ever talk about anything but those people at the diner anymore? I wish I could get a job there."

"No, Lily, you'd hate it," Doris said.

"That's what you said to Marybeth."

"Well, Marybeth does well because she's such a ray of sunshine," Doris said. "You go around frowning at everybody."

"I smile. Don't I smile, Marybeth?"

"Sure you do, Lily, but you'd be better off if you smiled a little more often," Marybeth admitted.

Lily practiced smiling. It tickled Marybeth to see Lily deliberately going out of her way to smile at people on the lane. In the supermarket she even overcame her shyness enough to talk to strangers. It was obviously a conscious effort, and Marybeth was impressed with Lily's determination.

"When school starts this fall," Lily said, "I'm going to have friends around me like you."

"You will," Marybeth assured her. Lily was no longer an emotional thirteen-year-old with hair-trigger sensitivities. She didn't cry over small hurts anymore. At fourteen Lily was still shy, but the strength of her character was showing through. "You have a wonderful smile, Lily."

For herself, Marybeth was pleased at her new friendship with her mother, glad that Doris took pride in the good things people said about her daughter at work. Her longing for Peter was with her as only a low-level pain, a dull throbbing on nights when she lay awake unable to sleep. Then she fantasized how it would be at the end of the summer when Peter returned from Alaska with a new outlook. "What I learned from the wilderness," he would say to her then, "what I learned is that you're more important to me than anybody, Marybeth. We're going to be together again from now on." They had never been separated for so long before. It had to mean he would be different when she saw him next. A summer in the empty tracts of Alaska would surely be enough to make a man out of him. "Now I know what love means, Marybeth," he said in her dreams. She had only to wait through the summer.

Garth Frazier was seeing a woman. Saturday nights if Marybeth wasn't called to fill in for somebody at the diner, she babysat with Lise and Eric. The sitter Doris had found for Garth was still with them daytimes. Garth said she was perfect, a warm, grandmotherly lady of seventy-odd years living on social security and still vigorous. She needed the extra income and enjoyed the children and the sense of being useful. Garth had a better job and was earning enough now to get by with one job, though his hours were long. He managed a garage for an owner who spent most of his time running another operation. Marybeth had only seen Garth's woman once—shoulder-length dark hair and too much flesh to be in style. She wasn't so beautiful as Laura, but she looked kind. Marybeth wondered if the woman would become the next Mrs. Frazier. She knew the divorce had gone through and Garth was free because he had made sure to tell her as if he didn't want her to think he could be seeing another woman when he was still married.

One Saturday afternoon early in July, Marybeth went over to babysit. She opened the unlatched screen door and walked into the Fraziers' living room calling, "Hi, everybody. I'm here."

Lise and Eric came running to greet her. Garth appeared at the top of the stairs in pants and a white dress shirt. His face was flushed and his blond hair gleamed as he wrestled with a tie.

"Marybeth, you don't know how to tie one of these things, do you?"

She laughed. "Not me. We don't have too many ties over at my house."

He grinned. "I guess not."

"You look so handsome!" she said.

"Going to a wedding. Nobody I know. I mean, they're not my friends; they're hers. I hate wearing ties. Last time I had to tie a noose like this was for my own wedding." He disappeared into the bedroom. A few minutes later he came downstairs with tie knotted and jacket on. "How do I look? . . . Like somebody not used to wearing a jacket and tie, right?"

"You look beautiful. You could pose for an ad," she said with genuine admiration.

His grin made him look more like sixteen than twenty-six. "Thanks. Trust you to make me feel good if anyone could." He stopped fussing with his cuffs and gave her a penetrating look. "Marybeth, can I ask you a personal question?"

"Sure."

"How come you're always available for babysitting on Saturday nights?"

"Well, because I'm not going out with anyone. Peter's gone for the summer. He went to Alaska. . . ."

Of course, I didn't see him too much when he was around—not for a while." Her voice trailed off.

"And doesn't a pretty girl like you get asked out by other boys?"

"I guess I'm sort of stuck on Peter."

"Sitting around waiting for him isn't a good idea. You should be out having fun—now—when you don't have too many responsibilities."

"You sound like Mama."

"Sorry."

"No, it's nice you care about me enough to want to give me advice."

"Oh, I care about you all right," he said. "Don't ever doubt that."

She looked at him directly to see what the undertone in his voice meant, but he dropped his eyes and went back to tugging at his shirt cuffs. "You know what I was thinking?" he said.

"What?"

"How'd you like me to teach you how to drive this summer?"

"You mean it?"

"You said your mother's too nervous, and you can't afford a school. I could do it, if you'd like to learn."

"I would," she said, "but you're going to be sorry if you try to teach me. I'll be an awful student."

"Let's start tomorrow." He looked as if he liked the idea.

He said goodbye to his children, who were so eager to get Marybeth's attention that they let him go without a fuss. "That boyfriend of yours," Garth said over his shoulder, "is an idiot not to appreciate you." He was out the door before the compliment sunk in. Then she could hardly believe he had said it. She liked Garth very much she realized. He had become like a strong, sweet, big brother living across the street, and it pleased her to know that he liked her too.

As she predicted, she was stupid about driving. She got so nervous every time she saw anything on the road ahead of her that she overreacted. The first day they went out of the lane onto the highway, she nearly drove the car into a ditch because a dog crossed the road.

"I can't drive. It's no use!" she wailed, taking her hands off the wheel and burying them in her lap.

"You're just starting. It's normal to make mistakes. Relax," Garth said.

"What do I need to drive for? I don't want to go anywhere anyway."

"You're going to be a senior this year. After you graduate, you have to look for a job. You only going to look somewheres you can walk to? That's just the post office and the firehouse and the church. You planning on being a preacher?"

Marybeth laughed. "Postmistress maybe. Fire-fighter? . . ."

He smiled. "Suppose you decide to take courses at the community college; who's going to drive you?"

"You could maybe," she teased.

"Marybeth, I'd do just about anything for you, but I'm not around that much. Now let's stop fooling around. Shift into reverse and get us out of here."

He kept her at it, never losing patience with her, and as more and more time went by, she began to feel she had to learn to drive if only to reward him for trying so hard.

"You know what?" Lily said one day after she and Lise and Eric had gone along on one of the more successful driving lessons.

"What?"

"Garth likes you."

"I know that."

"No, I mean he really *likes* you."

"Oh, Lily! Don't be silly. Garth is a grown man."

"Well, you're seventeen, Marybeth."

Marybeth frowned. Garth was still seeing the plump woman. Lily was just making things up in her romantic head.

Garth was in and out of the Mason house so frequently, he began to seem like a member of the family. Either he came after his children, who had taken to running over to the Masons' as if it were an extension of their own front yard, or he came because something had broken down and Doris had called him. Marybeth was surprised to see Doris so friendly with Garth. "How come you're so nice to him, Mama?" Marybeth asked. After all, Garth was a man.

"I like him, that's all," Doris said. "He's all right. You won't find him running out on anything. I was waiting on a teacher I had in high school the other day. She's retired now. She asked after Garth because she knows he lives on the bluff too. He was a favorite of hers. She said he was one of the finest boys she ever had, and how rough he had it being the youngest in that family of his."

In August Doris was sewing some fall clothes for Marybeth. Garth was downstairs looking at the Masons' ailing water heater. Marybeth thought the new dress emphasized her hips, which were already larger than she liked.

"Garth," Doris called. "You come up here and tell Marybeth how *you* think she looks in this dress."

Garth tromped upstairs, stripped to the waist and carrying a wrench. "She looks beautiful. But to me she looks beautiful in everything," he said.

"A lot of help you are," Doris grumbled.

But the strangest sensation came over Marybeth

when she saw him standing there with the muscles prominent on his bronzed shoulders and arms, and the winged eyebrows flying on his forehead. It was distinctly a sexual thrill and it embarrassed her. Peter had been gone too long, she thought. The makedo substitutes were't satisfying her enough—the touching and stroking and rubbing and pressing herself in bed at night only made her hungry for real lovemaking. But Peter would return in a few weeks, just a few weeks more.

"Before I graduate, I'm going to the senior ball with Peter. It'll be my last chance ever to wear a long dress and go to a dance like that," Marybeth said dreamily to Lily one evening when she was lying in the hammock Garth had installed for them in the backyard. "Peter will take me and I'll wear an ice-blue formal, with just little straps, or maybe with a halter neck, but anyways it will be blue, and he'll give me a corsage, and we'll dance all night, and it'll be just like when we used to walk through the halls together and nobody else mattered."

"Maybe he won't take you," Lily said.

"Oh, Lily! He'll be different when he comes back. You'll see."

"He won't be any different."

"You used to love Peter," Marybeth reminded her.

"Not anymore."

Marybeth looked at her sister. Lily wasn't a little girl anymore. She had slimmed down some and showed breasts and a waist. It was hard to tell she had any handicap, she covered it so well. She spoke as clearly as anyone now, and her limp was only evident when she tried to hurry. This would be a good year for Lily too. Marybeth felt sure of it.

She didn't know exactly when Peter was due to return. The two postcards he had sent her didn't say.

She guessed it was hard to tell how much ground the van was going to cover since it was always breaking down on them in inconvenient places. So she wasn't surprised when the phone rang and it turned out to be Peter already home.

"Marybeth?"

"Peter!" she screamed.

"You got to come over here fast. I need help."

"What's the matter?"

"I got home last night, and this morning my grandmother died on us."

Chapter 12

As he stood there in his grandparents' entry hall, he looked older all right. The bags under his eyes and two inches of scraggly beard in a semicircle under his mouth took care of that. He took her in his arms silently and hugged her, rocking her back and forth in a lingering embrace. "Marybeth, I don't know what to do," he said.

"Poor Peter. What an awful homecoming for you. How's your grandfather taking it?"

"He's acting queer. He called our minister, and he called the funeral parlor all right, but now he's just walking around and around like he doesn't know what

147

to do with himself. I made breakfast for him this morning, but he didn't get the idea that he was suppose to sit down and eat. He just looked at me and at the food, and he asked if he was supposed to clean up—like he didn't understand what the eggs were on the plate there for."

"Did he eat anything?"

"No."

"He's in a state of shock. It'll pass, Peter. But he shouldn't be alone. People will probably start coming by soon. That'll be good for him. And probably people will bring you food and stuff so you won't have to cook anything. Anyway, I'll bring over your dinners for tonight. But you better not leave him alone. Just keep after him talking and try to get him to eat."

She could feel him nod, the beard scratching up and down against her cheek. Then he released her so that he could look at her and he said, "My mother called. We haven't heard from her since Christmas. But when I told her that Grandma had died just like that in her sleep, she said she'd get on the next plane out here."

"Oh, that's good. That's the best news. Isn't it?"

"I don't know. I haven't seen her in so long. I don't know if I want to see her. Now you better tell me. What am I supposed to be doing for now?"

"Just stick with your grandfather and answer the phone and the door and make people welcome."

She looked through the archway into the living room at the stiff-backed furniture with dark wine-and-blue upholstery studded with brass heads along the curved wooden arms and feet. Everything looked cared for, ready for company if a little on the forbidding side. His grandmother had spent all her time with a dustrag in her hands. Peter said it was his grandfather's joke that the smell of furniture polish was his grandmother's favorite perfume.

"Do you want me to look around the house and see if anything needs doing?" Marybeth asked.

"Yeah, sure. Go ahead."

He followed her as she checked the immaculate bathroom downstairs and the food supplies in the big old-fashioned kitchen. "Better get in some more coffee and tea when you get a chance," she told Peter. "Have you called the close relatives—the aunts and uncles and cousins and her friends too? They'll want to attend the funeral."

When the Josselyns' minister arrived, Marybeth left. Later Peter called her and said a woman from his grandmother's altar guild had come in and taken over. "But Marybeth," he said, "I've gotta get out of here. I'm getting claustrophobia. Can you go for a drive with me?"

"You shouldn't leave your grandfather alone, should you?"

"He doesn't even know I'm here. He just wanders around, and he listens to that woman from the church better than to me."

"Okay," she said. "Whatever you think." She thought he might be needing to talk about his grandmother, to express his grief. Whatever he needed, she wanted to be there for him.

They drove out into the countryside where small houses were surrounded by acres of land and farms maintained a precarious existence. Pure blue sky capped the sun-hazed trees, which cast pools of green shade where the cows rested peacefully. Death had no presence at all in the timeless setting.

"It's really beautiful around here, isn't it, Peter?"

"You think this is nice, you ought to see Mt. McKinley. Alaska is fantastic, Marybeth. You just can't believe those glaciers and the size of everything. It knocks your eyes out."

"Well, it's pretty here too."

"Yeah, it's okay, I guess. But don't you ever get tired of looking at the same stuff all the time?"

"No. I don't get tired of what I like."

"That's lucky for me, isn't it?" he said. The long-lashed brown eyes offered a humble gratitude, but it wasn't gratitude she wanted.

"I've been waiting for you to come back for so long, Peter."

"Well, I'm back, but I don't know." His eyes changed and evaded hers. "I thought Alaska was going to help me think through what I want to do with my life, you know? But I guess I was too busy soaking up new experiences to do much thinking. Anyway, I'm just as confused as before I left. Like this is my senior year, and I don't know if I want to apply to college or—Maybe I ought to be working with my hands. I just can't see myself four years from now is all. Grandpa always said I should be a doctor or a lawyer or something like that, and I could see it, being a doctor, having people look up to me like if I was thirty-five, you know? But now—it just doesn't seem possible. I've got this urge to chuck everything—school, work, and everything, and just take off and see the world. I mean, why not? Right? What's to hold me back?"

She caught her breath. Then breathing shallowly, she managed to say, "A couple of people need you around, Peter."

"Who?"

"Your grandfather and me. You can't desert him now. He doesn't have anybody else, and as for me—I can't keep on waiting and waiting. It hurts too much." Her fingers touched their familiar talisman. "Do you remember what you said when you gave me this heart?"

"No. . . . Marybeth, don't make me feel bad. You

always make me feel bad, and I can't help it. It's not like I want to hurt you."

"Then what do you want?"

"I told you. I don't know. I love you. You're my girl, but—"

"And love is just a feeling?" she asked quoting him.

"No. I know it means more than that but—"

"Do you think it's fair to leave me just sitting around waiting for you forever?"

He frowned and his eyes slid away from her. "Marybeth, I don't know what you should do. I don't know what *I* should do, so how am I going to know what *you* should do? I know I don't always treat you right. I know that. But what am I going to do about it? I'm not ready to get tied down. I just turned seventeen. It's crazy for me to think of getting married or something like that. I do love you, but you know, I'm not ready yet."

He stopped the car in the dry, dirt driveway of a small manufacturing plant, up for sale according to the sign. "Marybeth," he begged, holding his arms out to her. "I know I'm no good to you. But I need you now. Be good to me. Don't desert me now."

Automatically her body responded. Her arms went around him. His head was cradled against her neck. She stroked his cheek while his hands found the softness of her breasts and squeezed gently. Her eyes filled with tears. She wanted him so urgently, and he needed her, and she had already forgotten how unlike the words in her dreams what he actually said had sounded. "Oh, Peter," she said, and let all her anger and hurt at his failure to come back any different sink in the overpowering flood of desire. Their lovemaking left her drowned, too exhausted to think at all.

Peter's mother arrived for the funeral. Marybeth saw her standing beside Peter at the service. A theatrical-looking woman with red hair and exotic makeup in a clingy dress. Peter kept looking down at her as if she fascinated him. Marybeth stood in line with the fifty or so people who had attended the services, waiting to express her condolences to the family. When her turn came, she took Mr. Josselyn's hand between hers and told him how sorry she was. His blanked-out eyes didn't see her. He nodded as he was nodding at everybody. He looked pathetically thin and lost. Marybeth felt so sorry for him that she had to blink away tears as she turned to Peter's mother, who was next.

"I'm Marybeth Mason. I live down the lane from your parents," Marybeth said, looking curiously into the self-possessed face of Peter's mother. "It must be such a terrible shock to lose your mother suddenly like this."

"People get to a certain age and you begin to expect these things," Peter's mother said. "Though of course, it comes as a shock anyway." She smiled radiantly at Marybeth, Peter's smile. "Are you a friend of Peter?"

"Marybeth and I went through school here together," Peter said. "We've been friends for years."

Marybeth stepped on past his mother and stood in front of him. He was next in line. Why hadn't he introduced her as his girl? Unable to say a word, she accepted the hand he held out stiffly. When had she become just an old friend? She felt ashamed. His eyes wouldn't meet hers. "Peter?" she asked, but he looked over her shoulder at the next person in line, and she had to walk on out to the parking lot where she had left her mother's car. She sat in it shaking for a long time before she could drive herself home.

He had failed her again, but it *was* at his grandmother's funeral, and he was confused. What had she expected him to say? "Mother, this is my girl, Mary-beth"? That would have been enough, just the simple recognition of what was, not even a promise of what could be. But maybe he was embarrassed in front of all those people in the limelight of such a solemn occasion. Maybe he hadn't even realized what he was saying. A cold misery filled her to the brim. He had come back, but he wasn't any different.

That night he walked into her kitchen, where she stood drying dishes listlessly. "Marybeth, I need you to help me think this out."

She finished the last dish and dropped into a chair opposite him at the kitchen table. She stared at him sullenly.

"My mother wants me to go back to Arizona with her," he said.

"Now?"

"She says I need some perspective on my life. She says I've been cramped up here on this bluff with old people for too long. She says Phoenix would open me up."

"To what?"

"To what life's all about. I told you how I am, Marybeth. I'm all confused about what I want to do after high school. I can't make up my mind to anything. And she's so fast and sure—the way she talks. I really want to get to know her better. She's something, isn't she?"

"I wouldn't know."

He blinked at her anger, but ignored it. "See, the thing is, I really don't want to skip out on my senior year here. I mean, I know everybody here. And I'd like to stay and graduate with the kids I know."

"You can't leave your grandfather alone," she said.

"Oh him! He's so out of it, I can't believe it. I swear he doesn't even recognize me. It gives me the willies the way he wanders around picking things up and putting them down, not answering when you talk to him.''

"He needs someone to take care of him. He's in a state of shock. After all, they were married more than fifty years."

"Yeah, I know. But the way he is now, it doesn't matter who takes care of him. We could hire someone, a companion or something like that."

"Your mother thinks it's all right for you to leave him alone?"

"I'm telling you he wouldn't be alone, Marybeth."

"He'd be alone if no one he loves is with him."

"What you don't understand is, he doesn't care. It's not going to matter to him. I mean, he's a tough old bird, Marybeth."

"He took care of you when you needed him."

"Only because he had to. All I was was a burden on him."

"I don't think that's true."

"How do you know? I mean, really, Marybeth, you don't know about him and me except what I told you. And the thing is, I never had a chance to get to know my mother, and now—I think I want to go to Phoenix with her."

"You think she's changed?"

"From what? You mean because she's never bothered with me much? She said she thought it was better not to interfere, to let them bring me up the way they thought best. She says she thought they'd make better parents than she could be to me."

"And now it's different?"

"When she walks into a room, everything comes alive. She's so full of life, and that's the way it is out there, she says. I'm sick of being cooped up in this musty little dead end. I want to go where I can breathe free and easy."

"Except your responsibility is here," she said firmly. "Your grandfather does love you even if he doesn't make a big fuss over you. He always gave you everything you said you wanted, and he tried to raise you right. You can't just turn your back on him and walk out now."

He fiddled with the fork on the table. "Maybe I'll ask him if he wants me to stay," he mumbled.

"You said he's confused. How's he going to answer you? If he tells you anything, it will probably be to go and do what you want, but that doesn't mean he wants you to go."

"You just don't know my grandfather. He really doesn't need anybody. He's a tough old bird."

"I don't know why you came here, Peter. Your mind's made up already."

"Maybe it is. I don't know." His beautiful eyes met hers, appealing for her sympathy. "I guess what I want is to ask you something, Marybeth. Will you wait for me till next June—just till then?"

"No," she said.

"Marybeth! What's the matter with you? You're not deserting me now? You can't. You're my girl."

"No, I'm not. Not anymore." She stared at him. What a baby he was the way he reached out for any loving he could get without any notion of how to love back. She could see that now. She could see him mouthing words at her, the puppy-dog eyes pleading, but she couldn't hear anything he said for the roaring in her ears. He took her hand but she pulled it loose. Finally he stood up to go.

"I'm coming back next June. I'm gonna take you to the senior prom, Marybeth."

Chapter 13

After he left, her body reacted before her mind did. In quick succession she felt hot, then chilled, then swollen. Her feet found their way out of the house, across Garth's yard and down the tracing of path against the shoulder of the bluff. She stopped where the lopsided tree reached out to the river with half its roots bared to wind and water. She had waited for him faithfully. She had believed that her waiting had power. She had believed that he would grow up and match her waiting with his love. It could have happened. But the waiting had not been enough. Her love alone was not enough. The dream had failed, and now everything was ordinary. The river was just moving water too polluted to swim in. The leaves of the bushes were scraggly, dusted over with the dry end of summer, poor as her life was poor without him. What good was living if she couldn't hope anymore?

Automatically her eyes followed a floating branch that had one live cluster of leaves on an upthrust twig. It was drifting close to the shore which was littered with debris—a plastic fertilizer bag, smashed boards, beer bottles. If the branch touched shore and stuck then. . . . Her mind began its ritual of waiting. No, she told herself sharply. No. She was done with waiting.

No matter how empty it left her, she had done with it.

The river hurried by ceaselessly. No magic in its movement now. Branches hung sapless, and only a trickle remained of the burbling springtime brook. Something in the bushes made a scratching sound, but she wasn't curious enough to turn to see. She sat like a stone in the emptiness of loss.

"Marybeth!" Garth's voice startled her. She looked around. He was running toward her surefooted as she had never been on that tricky path. "Are you all right?" he asked. He examined her face as if he didn't expect her to be.

"What are you doing here, Garth?"

"Lily said he did something to you." Garth tossed his head to indicate Lily up near the top of the bluff, crouched like a bird of prey, peering down at them.

"Oh, Lily," Marybeth sighed.

"She thought you might be desperate."

"No, I'm not that crazy."

"I suspected you weren't."

"But you came anyway."

"Well, just in case."

"Thanks for coming to my rescue."

"I wish I could."

"What do you mean?"

"I wish I could make you forget that empty-headed kid. You've been suffering over him too long."

She remembered his wife, who had given him two children and left him. "I guess we can't help suffering."

The muscle in his jaw twitched. "No, but there should be an end to it sometime."

She nodded, wondering if she would finally come to the end.

"You know what Lily told me?" he said. "She said if you jumped into the river, she was going to jump in after you, and since you couldn't either of you swim, I better come save you both." He smiled so that Marybeth had to smile with him.

"Well, no need for anybody to get wet. I didn't come to jump, just to think," she said.

"And what have you been thinking?"

She held back for an instant. She wasn't used to confiding in him, but he was the best friend she had now. "Peter's going to Arizona," she said. Quite unexpectedly the tears spurted. "I don't know why I'm crying," she complained.

He put his hands on her shoulders and shook her gently. "Marybeth, listen to me. He never was worth a single hair on your head. He's just an ordinary kid."

"Well, what about me? I'm nothing special. I'm a river rat like Mama, and I don't even want to be anything else."

"You aren't ordinary."

"Yes, I am, Garth. I'm not very smart. I'm not very pretty. I don't have any special talent."

"Yes, you have."

"What?"

"You love. You love better than anyone I ever knew." His hand slid under her hair, and he rubbed the base of her skull in such a soothing way that Marybeth leaned into his strong fingers like a cat with her eyes half closed.

"He thinks he can come back and I'll be waiting for him. He said he'd take me to the senior ball. But I'm not going to wait."

"No. You start having fun now. As for that dance, it means a lot to you, doesn't it?"

"Well, I did want to go."

"Yeah, Lily told me. . . . Well, look, if by next June you aren't seeing any guy you want to go with, I'll take you to the dance."

"You'd go to a high school dance with me?"

"Why not?"

"You wouldn't feel funny about it?"

"I don't give a damn about what people think, if you mean because I'm too old—unless it would embarrass you to go with me, Marybeth. I wouldn't want to embarrass you."

"Me? I don't care what people think. I never did. But I know how you hate getting dressed up."

"Didn't I tell you I'd do anything for you? That includes putting on a tie." His eyes twinkled. "Also you might be surprised to discover I'm not such a bad dancer."

Marybeth studied his face. The way he was looking at her sent a curl of warmth into the cold center of her misery. "By next June you could be married," she said.

"I won't get married until you do."

"How do you know?" she asked.

"I just know. Come on." He touched her chin with one finger. "Let's get out of here now."

At home again, Marybeth unclasped the chain that held the heart Peter had given her and handed it to Lily. "You can have it if you want it."

"What did he do to you, Marybeth?"

"Nothing. I did it to myself."

"I told you I didn't like him anymore."

"You were smarter than me."

Some Saturday nights that fall if Marybeth wasn't going out with anybody, Garth took her to the movies or out bowling. He was so easy to be with that by December, Marybeth was turning down dates so that she'd be free to see Garth. She didn't have to invent conversation with him. She could just relax and say whatever came into her head. She liked talking to him, liked his laconic responses and the sensible remarks he made.

"Can't you find anyone better to take you out?" Doris grumbled as the evenings with Garth multiplied.

"What do you mean, 'better,' Mama?"

"More your own age."

"You always complained Peter was such a kid."

"But Garth Frazier is too old for you."

"Less than ten years. That's not much between a man and a girl. You said that yourself."

"I never said any such thing. The point is he's not the kind to just fool around with. He's got to be looking for someone who'll take over where his wife left off, and you're too young to take on that kind of burden."

"Am I, Mama?"

"Marybeth, you're not thinking of settling down with a man with two children, are you? A grease monkey with no prospects?"

"Sounds awful." Marybeth smiled, trying to make light of it.

"Well, it certainly does—a young girl like you. Now that you're done with that flyweight down the road, I thought you might get some sense finally and make something of yourself."

"Garth wants me to register at the community college after I graduate high school. There's a nursing program I might try."

"Now you're talking. That's more like it."

"But Mama—"

"What?"

"If I fell in love with a man who had two children, that wouldn't stop me from marrying him, and if I cared about the children as much as I do about Lise and Eric, I'd be glad to wind up as their mother."

"Stepmother—and what do you know about that?"

"I could learn. I think I'd be good at something like that."

"You're impossible, Marybeth. I don't know what to do with you. You and Lily. You both act like you're too grown up to need me anymore. I might as well give up being your mother."

"We still need you, but maybe it is time you started thinking about yourself some. Maybe you should sign up for courses at the community college with me."

"At my age? Don't be silly."

"Everybody can change—at any age. Why not you, Mama?"

That January the river froze so hard it was safe for skating. Neighbors who hadn't seen each other for years met skating on the river and, with a hearty good cheer, compared the winter to the one fifteen years before when the ice had frozen like this. Garth got skates for Lise and Eric and Marybeth too. They skated almost daily. Garth skimmed the ice gracefully with Marybeth and the children trailing behind him bent-ankled and awkward, falling and giggling and having a marvelous time. In the spring, when the ice began breaking loose to melt and flow away, the good news came that the river was less polluted than it had been.

"Maybe we could buy a powerboat secondhand and go out on the river this summer," Garth said. "Would you like that, Marybeth? Would you like to go picnicking to some island? We could even go through the locks maybe. The kids would be excited about that."

"Me too," Marybeth said. The tenderness in his eyes when he looked at her melted something painful in her. To him, at least, she was someone special. In exchange, she took credit because his grim look had gone. Being the source of his happiness made her proud.

She wore the ice-blue formal she had imagined for the senior ball, and Garth's admiration turned her into a proper princess. She didn't care that he was a grown man at a dance where all the other girls had brought boys. All that mattered was the way he held her, as if she were precious, the only girl in the room in his eyes.

Hillary came in late with her tennis star boyfriend. She made a grand entrance in a fiery red dress that provoked attention. To Marybeth's amazement, Hillary's roving eyes stopped their sweep of the room to study Garth. Then the music began and Marybeth forgot Hillary for the dancing. Garth's natural grace made him an excellent dancer. He moved as if he were inside the rhythms.

"I'm so glad you took me, Garth," she said. "I'm having a wonderful time."

He smiled, concentrating on the music. Between numbers, they were standing at the side of the dance floor when Hillary's voice said, "I see you took my advice."

"What?" Marybeth turned around.

"You know what I told you," Hillary said. "Aren't you going to introduce me?"

Marybeth made the introductions without enthusiasm. She didn't recall any advice Hillary had given her, nor did she care enough to ask what it had been. She watched Hillary giving her animated all to the story of the car trouble that had made her and her date late to the dance. Garth listened politely, smiling, but when the music started again, he said,

"Nice meeting you," and led Marybeth back onto the dance floor.

"That was the girl Peter—" Marybeth began.

"I know," Garth said shortly.

When Marybeth saw how Hillary's eyes followed Garth around the dance floor, she was amused, even more amused later when Hillary whispered to her. "He's smashing, Marybeth. Wherever did you find him?"

"I think he found me," Marybeth said.

Halfway through the evening they walked toward the refreshment table to get some punch, and there stood Peter watching her. Her fragile new structure of happiness wavered and threatened to come crashing down. It was Peter standing there, her Peter, the boy she had loved since sixth grade. The wistful look on his face twisted in her. She took a step toward him. Garth's hand tightened on her arm. "Marybeth!" he warned.

"I just want to say hello. It's Peter."

He looked at her as if she had betrayed him or was about to, but she only saw the look later as an after-image in her mind. Now he was just a stranger standing in her way. She sidestepped him and hurried to greet Peter with a kiss on his cheek.

"How have you been?" she asked him gladly.

"I told you I'd take you to the prom, Marybeth. Didn't you believe me?"

"Peter! You didn't even write."

"I tried to get you on the phone, but you weren't home. Anyways, why did you come with *him?*"

Marybeth's eyes went from Peter's flushed face to find Garth, who had moved out of earshot allowing privacy for her reunion. His strong fingers were drumming on the refreshment table in time to a band that wasn't playing now, and his eyes were fixed on a far distant point somewhere inside himself. She stared at him as if he were the one who had returned after an absence, seeing him suddenly—the promise of endurance in his jaw, the strength of his long limbs, the pride and the beauty in him. She stood there with her mouth open seeing for the first time what a man he was.

"Marybeth, what's the matter with you?" Peter asked. "Are you sick or something?"

"Good talking to you," she murmured with a distracted politeness. Then she walked back to Garth and took his hand.

"Dance one more dance with me," she said. "And then let's go home."

She looked away from the magic of the dark, flowing river and the incandescent moonlight. He was lying on one arm watching her. She wondered how long he had been awake and watching.

"What's the matter?" he asked.

"Nothing."

"You aren't sitting up this time of night for nothing. What are you thinking?"

"Just—about my life."

"And?" He sounded anxious as if he suspected she had regrets.

"And I can't remember how some things happened between you and me. For instance, do you remember? When was the first time you kissed me?"

"At your senior prom. I kissed you goodnight."

"Oh, I remember that. Yes, you did."

"You don't remember because you were so busy thinking about that kid at the time."

"No, I wasn't. That wasn't it. What I was doing was trying to keep you from knowing how much I liked it when you kissed me."

He held his arms out ready to end the conversation there. "Wait a minute," she said. "Since you're so good at remembering. Tell me. Did you ever come right out and ask me to marry you, Garth Frazier?"

She saw the lower half of his face split into a crescent-shaped grin. "It was your mother," he said.

"Mama?" Marybeth asked incredulously.

ABOUT THE AUTHOR

CAROLE S. ADLER was born in Rockaway Beach, Long Island and attended Hunter High School and Hunter College. She received her master's degree in Elementary/High School Education from Russell Sage College. After teaching Middle School English for eight years, Mrs. Adler decided to pursue her dream of publishing a novel for young readers. She has been writing since she was seven years old, but it wasn't until 1979 that her first novel was published: the award-winning *The Magic of the Glits*. Since then she has had a dozen children's books and three young adult novels published. *Down by the River* was inspired by Mrs. Adler's involvement in a children's shelter tutoring 14–16-year-old girls, and expresses her views on love and marriage. The author tries to write four to five hours a day and loves to play tennis, her favorite sport, "to get away from the typewriter!" She and her husband live in Schenectady, New York.

Wouldn't It Be Great To Be In Love!

To have someone special, someone to laugh with, someone who loves you even when everyone else doesn't seem to care.

We have some books you're really going to love. For dreams that come true and wonderful stories of romance, curl up with one of these.

BOYS! BOYS! BOYS! by Jan Gelman 46730/$1.95

CUPID COMPUTER by Margie Milcsik 45290/$1.95

DON'T TELL ME THAT YOU LOVE ME by Hila Colman 44593/$1.95

I'LL ALWAYS REMEMBER YOU . . . MAYBE by Stella Pevsner 49416/$2.25

LOVE IS LIKE PEANUTS by Betty Bates 56109/$1.95

SEVENTEENTH SUMMER by Maureen Daly 44386/$2.50

THIS TIME COUNT ME IN by Phyllis Anderson Wood 42689/$1.95